It wasn't going to be easy . . .

Jennifer and I were already halfway through our ice-cream floats when Tessa and Andrea arrived. Tessa gave us a tight-lipped smile and slid into the bench across from us. Andrea sat down next to her and took out her yellow legal pad. She read:

"We, the undersigned, Jennifer Barnes and Tessa Ramsey, hereby agree to set aside our differences and be nice to each other for one week. During such time, we shall take all necessary actions to ensure that the friendship between Tessa's mother and Jennifer's father doesn't get *any* friendlier."

Jennifer's face was grim as she signed. "Agreed."

Tessa added her flowing signature and nodded shortly. "Agreed."

Andrea and I let out deep breaths. The truce had begun.

Ask your bookseller for these other JENNIFER titles:

YOU'RE CRAZY Jennifer!

Melanie Friedman

SPLASH™

A BERKLEY / SPLASH BOOK

JENNIFER #3, YOU'RE CRAZY, JENNIFER!, is an original publication of The Berkley Publishing Group. This work has never appeared before in book form.

A Berkley Book / published by arrangement with
General Licensing Company, Inc.

PRINTING HISTORY
Berkley edition / March 1991

A GLC BOOK

Splash and *Jennifer* are trademarks of
General Licensing Company, Inc.
Cover logo and design by James A. Lebbad.
Cover painting by Jaime DeJesus.

ISBN: 0-425-12605-6
RL: 5.6

A BERKLEY BOOK® TM 757,375
Berkley Books are published by The Berkley Publishing Group,
200 Madison Avenue, New York, New York 10016.
The name "BERKLEY" and the "B" logo
are trademarks belonging to Berkley Publishing Corporation.

PRINTED IN THE UNITED STATES OF AMERICA

10 9 8 7 6 5 4 3 2 1

YOU'RE CRAZY

Jennifer!

Chapter 1

"Willi's stalling! Disqualify her," cried a voice from the Blue Team on the other side of the room.

It was Tessa Ramsey, my arch-enemy. She was the Blue Team Captain, and she was trying to make trouble for me.

"No, I'm not!" I snapped back in self-defense. "I've still got time."

"She's cheating, Mr. Karch!" Tessa screamed, pointing to the face of her wristwatch. "Her time's up!"

"You're the one who's trying to cheat!" shot back Jennifer Barnes, our Red Team Captain and my best friend. "You're not letting Willi think."

"Silence!" shouted Mr. Karch, our ninth-grade math teacher. "I'll decide who's right or wrong in this algebra class." He glanced down at his stopwatch, waited a few seconds, then gave it a click with his thumb. "*Now* your time is up, Wilhelmina," he said. "Do you know the answer to the problem?"

I checked the figures on my scratch pad. "Is it—is it thirty-three?" I said.

I waited nervously for Mr. Karch's reply. So did everybody else on our team. We were losing by two points in Mr. Karch's monthly Math Bee. If I'd blown it, and the Blue Team could answer it correctly, we'd sink even further behind. In Gaylord ("Killer") Karch's class, the monthly Math Bee—held, without fail, on the first Thursday of every month—isn't just a game, it's a mental obstacle course that every freshman at Wanda McCoy Wellbie High School has to suffer through.

Mr. Karch rose from behind his desk and walked over to the windows, where our team was lined up. He stared down at me with his piercing gray eyes.

"Thirty-three, Wilhelmina?" he asked. "Is that your *final* answer?" I groaned inwardly. I *hate* it when teachers call me by my real name.

Now I was even less sure of myself. I knew there had to be a catch somewhere, but I didn't know where. I was positive I'd jotted down the problem exactly as Mr. Karch had read it out loud:

> "Jack" sold beans on weekends. On the first weekend, he sold half his beans to "Jill." On the following weekend, he sold half of the remaining beans to "Jill". If he had twenty-two beans left after the second weekend, what was the average number of beans he sold to "Jill"?

As far as I could tell, I'd done my arithmetic right. I still came up with the same number.

"Well," Mr. Karch asked. "We're all waiting."

As the cold March wind rattled the windows, I took a deep breath and said, "I'll stick with thirty-three."

"Well," Mr. Karch said, "I'm sorry, Willi, that's just not the correct answer."

A groan went up from my teammates. A cheer erupted from the other side of the room. Like the mighty "Casey" in "Casey at the Bat," I, Wilhelmina Jane ("Come Through in the Clutch") Stevens, had struck out.

"Blue Team!" Mr. Karch said, wheeling around. "For three points, can you give me the correct answer?"

It was Tessa's turn to answer for the Blues.

I prayed she wouldn't get it right. Aside from the obvious fact that I didn't want her team to get ahead five points because of my mistake, I had personal reasons for hoping that she would mess up. There has never been any love lost between Tessa Ramsey and me.

Last fall—right after Jennifer moved here to Wellbie, Iowa, from Boston and became my closest friend—Tessa had done everything she could to sabotage my budding romance with Robbie Wilton, the cutest boy in ninth grade. Fortunately, it didn't work. With Jennifer's help, I found a way to get Robbie to notice me more, and he wound up asking *me* to the Halloween Dance in October, *and* to the Valentine's Day Dance a couple of weeks ago. Tessa, who has a huge crush on Robbie, has never forgiven me—or Jennifer—for stealing Robbie away from her. If she didn't like me before

Jennifer Causewell Barnes blew into town, she certainly liked me even less now.

Tessa smirked and gave a haughty toss of her long red hair. "The correct answer," she said, throwing me a pointed look, "is thirty-three *beans per weekend.*"

"Precisely!" cried Mr. Karch, jumping for joy.

"WHAT?" I exclaimed in disbelief.

"WHAT?" cried the outraged Red Team.

An instant later, Jennifer was storming across the room toward Mr. Karch, her green eyes blazing.

"You can't allow that, Mr. Karch!" she complained angrily. "Willi's answer was right. The Red Team deserves those points. It's a tie game."

"No it's not, dearie!" snarled Tessa, jumping into the argument. "The score's nine to four. Willi forgot to add the part about *beans per weekend.*"

Jennifer held her ground. "Nobody took three points away from your team, *dreary*, when Fran Gerber answered 'eighty-eight square feet' instead of 'eighty-eight square feet *of wax paper.*' If Willi loses her points, Fran's got to lose hers, too."

"Ladies! Ladies!" Mr. Karch hollered. "Will you PLEASE return to your teams? There will be no further bickering during the Math Bee—or I will be forced to take drastic action!" He patted the vest pocket of his suit, where he kept his little black marking book.

"But, Mr. Karch—!" Jennifer began.

"GO!" Mr. Karch bellowed.

Jennifer and Tessa returned to their teams. Mr. Karch straightened his tie, cleared his throat, and

4

said, "MATH MUST MARCH ON! The score in the Math Bee is now nine to four. The Blue Team is winning."

A gasp of disbelief arose from our side. Jennifer lurched forward again, but I held her back—for her own good. Jennifer is a born crusader, a champion of the underdog. I love her for it, but it gets her, and me, into big trouble. Like last winter, when she launched a one-girl campaign against "Dear Heart," the anonymous advice columnist in *The Real McCoy*, our weekly school newspaper. She even set up a rival advice service of her own, called "Jennifer's Corner." How could she have known that "Dear Heart," whose advice Jennifer so often disagreed with, was none other than *me*, Willi Stevens?

Nobody is supposed to know I write that column, except Andrea Wellbie, the editor-in-chief, and Mr. Purdy, my English teacher and our newspaper adviser. It's my biggest secret in the whole world. Eventually, thank heaven, Jennifer abandoned the crusade that was causing me so much private grief. My column remained in the paper, and my secret identity was preserved. But Jennifer's impulsiveness and headstrong nature had nearly ruined our friendship.

"Now, are you ready, Red Team?" Mr. Karch asked.

"Yes, we're ready," Jennifer hissed through clenched teeth.

"And whose turn is it?" Mr. Karch asked.

"M-mine," a tiny mouselike voice stammered from behind me. It was Emma Guffey, the smallest and quietest girl in ninth grade and (unfortunately for us) one of the worst math students ever. There was no way she was going to be able to answer a "Killer" Karch three-point question. Already I could hear her knees knocking together in sheer terror.

"Listen carefully, Emma," Mr. Karch began as he reached for a question card from one of the piles on his desk.

"I think I'm going to faint," Emma whispered in my ear.

I turned around. Emma's face was as white as a sheet. It always turned that shade of white just before she fainted. Emma fainted a lot in school—whenever she was under stress.

"Oh, no! Don't faint now, Emma," I pleaded softly. But it was too late.

"Here I gooo . . ." Emma said, her eyelids fluttering.

Luckily, Robbie was standing on the other side of Emma and had seen her starting to sag. He immediately grabbed Emma's left arm. I grabbed her right.

I looked up in panic, but Mr. Karch wasn't even facing us. He wasn't aware that Emma had temporarily checked out of the Math Bee, and I suddenly saw why.

Unbeknownst to us, Mr. Buxton, our principal, had slipped into the classroom and was standing in the far corner by the door. He was gesturing wildly to catch Mr. Karch's attention.

"Mr. Buxton," Mr. Karch said, approaching him. "Is there something I could do for you? We're in the middle of our monthly Math Bee. Maybe you'd care to take a seat and watch."

Mr. Buxton shook his head.

"No, Mr. Karch. But I'd like to have a word with you if I could—*outside*."

"Certainly, Mr. Buxton," Mr. Karch replied.

At the doorway, Mr. Karch turned briefly to our class and said, "We'll pause the Math Bee until I return. Emma, you're up next, remember."

I placed my hand behind Emma's head and nodded it up and down like a puppet's. Thank heaven, Mr. Karch didn't notice!

Mr. Karch followed Mr. Buxton out into the hall. From inside the classroom, we could hear the sounds of two men whispering. Then we heard footsteps padding down the corridor.

In the meantime, Emma blinked awake to find Robbie and me supporting her like crutches. She looked at us with embarrassment and thanked us for keeping her from falling down. But her embarrassment changed to delight when we told her that Mr. Karch had been called out of the room and that she'd been given a temporary reprieve from humiliation.

Minutes passed. Where was Mr. Karch?

Finally, Jennifer spoke up. "It's ridiculous waiting here like this," she said. "I'm going to see if they're down the hall."

"Don't!" cried Jim Ellis, Jennifer's sort of boy-friend and Robbie's best friend. "What if Gaylord's waiting in ambush to see if somebody comes out?" Jim, who's as tall as a beanpole, raised his hands over his head like a cat about to pounce. "What if this is one of his devilish plots to drop us a grade or something?"

"C'mon, Jim," Jennifer replied. "There's only five minutes left in the period. We couldn't continue with the Bee even if Mr. Karch walked in right now."

Jennifer went over to the door and peeked down the corridor. "Relax, everybody," she said. "The hall's clear. They're gone."

With a feeling of relief, we all drifted back to our seats and waited for the bell that would end seventh period—and the school day.

"You know, this isn't like Gaylord," said Jim, who's the smartest kid in ninth grade. "He hates leaving his classes unsupervised. Mr. Buxton must have wanted him for something real important. Don't you wish you knew what?"

A light bulb went on in my head. "I know what it is," I said. "Mr. Karch is a nominee for that Iowa 'Math Teacher of the Year' award. It's been in all the papers. It's a real big deal. I bet Mr. Buxton wanted to see him about that."

"Do you think if he gets an award, he'll be any easier on us?" asked Bucky Armbruster, who's almost as bad at math as Emma. Last fall, Bucky, whose father owns the biggest farm in town, had a huge, secret crush on Jennifer and had even writ-ten letters to "Dear Heart" about her. Through my column, I managed to persuade him to try pursuing other girls, because the notion of Jennifer going out with the sweet but bumbling Bucky was just too ridiculous for words.

"Before anybody gives him an award, they ought to spend a week in our class," Jim said. "Maybe they'd reconsider."

Everybody laughed.

The bell rang and we were all free to leave. Jennifer and I headed for our lockers in the language arts building.

An icy wind swirled up from the golf course that neighbors the school and whipped our hair around. Our breath seemed to steam out of our mouths as we trudged along the outdoor path.

"I just couldn't believe what Mr. Karch did today," Jennifer said, shaking her head. "He was really off the wall. He practically *gave* points away to Tessa's side."

Even though I was still angry about Tessa's having gotten the better of me, I'd cooled off a bit. I couldn't agree with Jennifer that Mr. Karch had been totally unfair. "Look," I said. "You know how picky he is. He wants every answer perfect, down to the last 'bean per weekend.'"

"Yeah, I know," Jennifer said. "I just think he ought to learn to be a little more human. He's like a math machine, a computer without a heart."

I stopped short. Jennifer's remark reminded me of something. I wondered if I should let her in on a little surprise about this week's issue of the school newspaper, which was coming out tomorrow. In addition to secretly writing "Dear Heart" for the paper, I'm also *The Real McCoy*'s copy manager. So I knew all the articles that Andrea Wellbie had planned for tomorrow's issue. Andrea is a ninth-grader, like Jennifer and me, but she already has the mark of greatness stamped on her. She's the youngest editor of *The Real McCoy*—ever. And she's the fabulously wealthy great-granddaughter of Wanda McCoy Wellbie, the legendary founder of the world-famous Wellbie Cookie Company, and the person after whom our town and high school are named. She's also (I'm sorry to say) Tessa Ramsey's best friend.

Last week Andrea had okayed an article that I was sure would warm the hearts of all the many Karch-sufferers in school, Jennifer included.

"Actually," I said, "there may be a little justice left in the world. Math doesn't always 'march on' mechanically, like a machine."

"What do you mean?" Jennifer asked.

"Well, you know Lance Kirkwood's column?"

"Uh-huh. He writes 'Trivia On Toast,' the humor column."

"Right. Well, his next piece is about Mr. Karch. Andrea was swamped with work this issue, so she gave it to me to edit."

"Lance wrote a humor piece about Mr. Karch?" Jennifer asked.

"Uh-huh. Only, it's actually more like a poison-pen article."

"You mean, Karch finally gets his?" Jennifer asked.

"Yup," I said. "Lance did a real number on him. Andrea's hoping that it'll shock Mr. Karch. Make him sit up and take notice—the way Scrooge got shocked in *A Christmas Carol*."

"Oooh, I can't wait to read it," Jennifer said gleefully. "I'm going to frame it and hang it on my wall."

"So will everybody else," I said. "It could create a big stir."

We continued walking. The cold had begun to turn Jennifer's cheeks red. Her face glowed with an inner radiance. She's so beautiful—so naturally beautiful. It's easy to see why she'd been a success-ful teenage model—*Dazzle* magazine's "Cover Girl of the Year"—before she'd moved to Wellbie. That was another reason Tessa hates Jennifer. She can't stand the fact that Jennifer is prettier than she is and that practically all the boys in school—even the seniors!—were just dying to date her.

"You know, Willi," Jennifer said. "It's a good thing that Andrea is starting to give you other assignments, like editing. You're much too talented a writer to stay a stupid copy manager. You should be doing other things—like serious reporting."

I sighed. "That's my dream. I'm just waiting for Andrea to give me my big break."

"Maybe she's starting to come around," Jennifer said. "She let you edit Lance's article."

"That's true," I said.

"Speaking of which," Jennifer said with a touch of mischief in her voice, "you wouldn't happen to have an advance copy on you, would you?"

11

"No, I wish I did," I said. "The paper's at the printer's right now. You, me, and everybody else will have to wait until tomorrow. Then we'll see how well Mr. Karch can take a joke."

Chapter 2

The next morning, when I got to school, I could tell instantly that Lance's column had made a big hit. My first clue was when Robbie Wilton dashed out of his homeroom into the hall and grabbed hold of Jim Ellis, who was trying to stuff his heavy overcoat into his too-small locker.

"You gotta read this!" Robbie howled as he shoved the paper into Jim's face.

"I'm going to have to eat it if it gets any closer," replied Jim, pushing Robbie's hand away.

"No, c'mon Jim, take a look," Robbie persisted. "See—over here, in Lance's column. It's all about Gaylord."

Jim seized the newspaper from Robbie. Soon, he'd forgotten all about his coat, and was laughing so hard he was starting to cry.

"Hey, guys!" Jennifer greeted the two laughing figures. "Mind if I take a look at your paper?"

Jim glanced at Jennifer and tried to speak, but another wave of laughter hit him. "Here," he gasped, handing her his newspaper, "I-I can't talk now." He and Robbie looked at each other and burst into laughter again.

Jennifer's eyes scanned the page and widened in amazement as she read the headline on Lance's article aloud: "GAYLORD KARCH FIRED FROM MATH DEPARTMENT, REPLACED BY ROBOT." She gave me a quizzical look and said, "This sounds like what I was saying yesterday—I mean, about Gaylord being some kind of math machine."

I nodded.

Jennifer read on, breaking into laughter. "Just listen to this, Willi," she howled.

> "We decided to hire the robot," school officials said, "because we knew it would never make a mistake and also because it was friendly to kids and it didn't force the cooks in the lunchroom to make three bacon cheeseburgers for it every day." Students said they like their new electronic teacher a lot because it doesn't hold Math Bees and it plays neat video games with them during their study halls.

"You like that part, huh?" I said. "The video games were my idea."

Jennifer didn't hear me. "Oh, and get this," she said.

> Asked why Mr. Karch had been fired, school officials said that they'd discovered that Mr. Karch's college records were

incomplete. He'd never actually finished two courses, Basket Weaving 101 and Advanced Frisbee Throwing, that were *the* basic requirements for a teaching position at Wellbie High. The robot, on the other hand, had gotten A+'s in both courses.

I winced a little as Jennifer read those lines. I'd tried to get Lance to soften them a bit because I thought he was being too harsh on Mr. Karch. But he'd insisted on keeping them in as written.

By the time Jennifer had finished the article, she was a total wreck. And in every homeroom we passed, the story was exactly the same. Kids were laughing and yelling to each other: "Hey, you gotta read what Lance wrote about Karch!" or "Hey, did you check out 'Trivia on Toast'?" Andrea and I had thought that the article would make a big splash, but the reaction it was getting was even bigger than we'd expected.

When Jennifer and I walked into our homeroom, I looked for Andrea to tell her what a sensation Lance's column was making. But she wasn't in the room. I saw Tessa and Bucky, but no Andrea.

I was about to plunk my books down on my desk when Mademoiselle Paulette, our homeroom teacher, gazed up from her desk and motioned to me.

"Wilhelmina, *chérie*," she said in her lovely singsong voice.

"Yes?" I replied.

"*Venez ici*—come here. I have something for you." Mademoiselle Paulette, who's also my French teacher, is actually from Iowa, but she believes in living what she teaches.

When I reached Mademoiselle Paulette's desk, she handed me a pink slip with the chilling words . . . FROM THE PRINCIPAL'S OF-FICE . . . stamped across the top.

"Monsieur Buxton wants to see you at once!" she said.

I felt a sudden chill that had nothing to do with the weather.

"Uh-oh!" Jennifer said.

"Do you have any idea what he wants me for, Mademoiselle?" I asked.

Mademoiselle Paulette picked up the copy of *The Real McCoy* lying on her desk. "For this."

"Oh," I said.

"Good luck," said Jennifer as I passed her on my way out.

I had a major case of the butterflies as I trudged over to the administration building, where the principal's office is located. I wished I had Jennifer's courage. I'd never gotten into trouble with Mr. Buxton before for anything. Not for my grades or my behavior. Not for anything I'd done in my job as copy manager of *The Real McCoy*. Not even for the personal advice I'd given as "Dear Heart." But there was always a first time for everything, I guessed, and today appeared to be it for me.

I paused outside the administration building to

stare at my reflection in the big glass door. I was a sight. I'd left the house this morning in a hurry without brushing my hair. It was a tangle of mousy brown knots. My hazel eyes had dark circles under them from too little sleep. And my lips were chapped from the frigid weather we'd been having.

I took a minute to compose myself in my make-shift mirror, then yanked open the door and went inside.

When I got to the office, it was bustling with early morning activity. Turk Guffey, the school maintenance man (and Emma's dad), was standing inside the doorway on a paint-splattered stepladder, changing some fluorescent lights in the ceiling. Toward the middle of the room, behind a long oak counter, were two secretaries who were busy writing out late passes for a bunch of kids whose bus had broken down.

I didn't see Alice, Mr. Buxton's secretary, anywhere.

"Alice around?" I asked Turk.

Turk gestured toward a closed door with the words PRINCIPAL'S OFFICE printed on it in large gold letters.

"She's in there," he said. "Find a seat. There's one next to Lance."

I gulped. Talk about bad omens!

Lance Kirkwood, a short, runty-looking boy wearing thick, black-rimmed glasses and a frayed red baseball cap, was sitting on the detention bench, staring unhappily at his sneakers.

I plopped myself down beside him. Lance (better

known as "the Twerp") acknowledged my presence with a grunt.

"You waiting to see Mr. Buxton, too?" I asked.

Lance shook his head. "Nope. I've seen him already."

"What are you still doing here?"

"Alice has to give me a late pass."

I suddenly remembered which bench we were sitting on. "Did he give you detention?"

The Twerp shook his head again. "No, it's much more complicated than that."

"What do you mean?" I said.

"You'll see. You won't believe it when you hear it."

"Lance, what are you talking about?"

"You'll find out. But I didn't lie to you or Andrea about the column," he said. "I made the whole thing up out of my head. Just remember that."

The door to Mr. Buxton's office swung open and Alice emerged, carrying an issue of *The Real McCoy* in one hand and a steno pad in the other.

"Alice!" I called, hopping off the bench. "Mademoiselle Paulette told me Mr. Buxton wanted to see me about something."

"Yes, he does," Alice said. She ducked back into Mr. Buxton's office for a moment and mumbled something. Then she reemerged and said, "You can go in now, Willi."

I screwed up my courage and walked in.

A tired, tense-looking Mr. Buxton was standing in front of his desk, tapping a metal ruler against the palm of his hand. He was a large man with thinning, carrot-colored hair and deep set eyes.

Gazing around the room, I saw that three chairs had been arranged in a neat semicircle to the left of Mr. Buxton's desk. Sitting in two of the chairs were Andrea Wellbie and Mr. Purdy. Mr. Buxton motioned me to sit in the third one and got right to the point.

"Andrea," he began, "you've been editor of the school newspaper about how long now?"

"Six months, sir, I guess," Andrea replied.

"And Willi," he said, turning to address me, "your job is what on the paper?"

"I'm the copy manager, sir. All the articles have to go through me first."

"I see," Mr. Buxton said. "But that's not your *only* responsibility, right?"

I shot a look at Andrea. I wondered if she'd been forced to tell Mr. Buxton about "Dear Heart."

"I mean," Mr. Buxton continued, "from what Andrea tells me, the two of you share responsibility for assigning and editing some stories. Am I correct?"

My secret was safe after all.

"Yes sir, that's correct," I replied.

"Good, I'm glad we've got that straight. Now, I've asked both of you—and Mr. Purdy—to be here, because I want to discuss a grave matter with you."

"Yes, very grave," echoed Mr. Purdy, who betrayed his own nervousness by combing his hair up over his bald spot with his fingers. Under normal circumstances, he would never have done that in public.

Mr. Buxton leaned forward toward Andrea and said, "During all the time you've been editor, Andrea, have I ever interfered with what you've written or chosen to print?"

"No, Mr. Buxton," she said. "You've been really great about that."

"I'm glad to hear you say that," he said. "Because I think I've been pretty tolerant too, more so than most principals. But when it comes to something like this"—Mr. Buxton turned and lifted a copy of *The Real McCoy* off his desk—"I'm afraid I have to draw the line."

I squirmed in my seat, and I could see that Andrea was becoming more and more uncomfortable, too.

Mr. Buxton dropped the newspaper back onto his desk with Lance's column facing up. He stood over Andrea, tapping the ruler in the palm of his hand. "This article—'Trivia on Toast'—is an example of totally irresponsible journalism. I want to know why you printed it."

"It was just a joke, Mr. Buxton," Andrea said with an anxious laugh. "That's what Lance's column is all about. He pokes fun at things."

"I know what Lance writes, Andrea. But in this case it's not very funny, and it's no joke."

"But Mr. Buxton," I said, "a lot of teachers have been roasted by Lance before. It's almost an honor to be in his column. Mr. Purdy got roasted last December."

Mr. Purdy's face reddened. "I must tell you, I didn't like the part about my flying to Nepal for a wig."

Mr. Buxton went on. "Tell me, did either of you question Lance about what he wrote, or check his facts?"

"No, sir," Andrea said. "It's fiction. There aren't any facts. He just makes everything up."

"He told you that, eh?" Mr. Buxton said, stroking his chin. "Well, do you know if he interviewed Mr. Karch or anybody else?"

"No, that would have spoiled the surprise," I said.

"And is that why you didn't inform Mr. Purdy?"

"Mr. Purdy didn't ask to read Lance's column," Andrea explained. "We didn't see any reason to show it to him."

"Is that true, Sam?" Mr. Buxton asked Mr. Purdy.

Mr. Purdy nodded. "Yes, I'm sorry, Larry," he said, wringing his hands.

Andrea spoke up next. "Mr. Buxton, neither Willi nor I have the faintest idea what this is all about. Why are you grilling us like this? We're sorry if you think Lance's column was in poor taste."

Mr. Buxton stared at Andrea for a long while, then at me. "Maybe you two really *don't* know what this is about," he said. "I'm talking about something far more serious than just bad taste, Andrea." He dropped his voice to a whisper and glanced at the door to make sure it was closed. "Your reporter—

Lance—appears to have gotten access to confidential information from secret school board meetings, and I believe he used that information as the basis of his story."

"Secret meetings?" I asked, bewildered.

Mr. Buxton furrowed his brows, then said, "Meetings that have been held over the past three weeks to decide whether Gaylord Karch should be dismissed."

"Whether WHAT?" Andrea exclaimed.

"You can't be serious," I said. "Dismissed? You mean fired?"

"I mean exactly that, Willi—just as the article says."

"Oh, c'mon, Mr. Buxton!" I said nervously. "Lance made everything up about Mr. Karch being fired."

Mr. Buxton wasn't smiling. "I wish he had, Willi. As of yesterday, the school board has ordered Mr. Karch temporarily suspended from teaching. A substitute teacher will be taking over your algebra class."

I nearly fell out of my chair. "Suspended? But why?" I asked. "What did he do?"

"I can't discuss the details," Mr. Buxton said wearily, "because the school board is still debating the matter. But I suggest you turn on your television tonight. I'm sure it'll be all over the evening news."

Andrea and I sat there, stunned.

Mr. Buxton circled back behind his desk and sat down. "Now here's the main reason I called both of you in," he said. "The school board will be meeting again over the next few weeks—mostly in secret session. I'm trusting you with this information because I need to have your promises that there will be no more leaks like this appearing in *The Real McCoy*, in jest or earnest. It's bad enough when I read unflattering stories about this school in the regular newspapers. I don't need to read them in my own school's newspaper! Am I making myself perfectly clear?"

I was in a bit of a daze. I vaguely remember answering something like "yes, sir" or "okay, sir." I have a hazy recollection of our being helped up and escorted out of Mr. Buxton's office by Alice.

Minutes later, Andrea and I found ourselves sitting on a wooden bench outside the administration building, staring dumbly into space.

"It was a joke, just a joke," I mumbled to Andrea.

"It was just one of his regular columns, right?" Andrea replied, with glazed eyes. "Lance told me he made it up. That Twerp couldn't have been lying to me, could he?"

I shrugged. The cold wind licked at my heels. I didn't know what to believe.

Chapter 3

I kept my promise to Mr. Buxton. When I returned to class, I didn't breathe a word to anyone about what he'd told us in his office. It wasn't easy, though, trying to keep a secret from Jennifer.

"You've gotta tell me everything," she whispered when we had our first free moment together in first-period gym class.

"I'm dying to tell you, but I can't," I said.

"Why not?"

"Because I promised I wouldn't. Mr. Buxton said not to say anything until the whole story came out tonight."

"What story?" Jennifer asked with exasperation. "All you've told me so far is that you and Andrea got into some kind of trouble over Lance's column. You haven't told me what." She gave me a hurt look. "I'm your friend. If you're in trouble, I've got a right to know—no matter what Bossy Buxton says."

"I know, Jennifer," I said. "But the truth is, I don't know all the details yet myself. All I know is what Mr. Buxton told us: that if we watched the six o'clock news, we'd get the whole story on Mr. Karch."

"What story on Mr. Karch?" Jennifer asked. "Do you mean there's going to be something on TV about Lance's story?"

My face reddened at my stupid slip of the tongue. "No, Jennifer, that's not what I meant. Please try to understand. Don't ask me any more questions—at least not for a couple more hours. Call me after the news. We'll talk then, okay?"

Seeing how much her questions were upsetting me, Jennifer finally agreed to back off and discuss the subject later on.

I breathed a sigh of relief. Jennifer and I are so different in temperament. I'm just not a rule-breaker or a rule-bender, like she is. I always play things boringly straight—whether it's a matter of dutifully keeping my promises to people or faithfully keeping other people's secrets. I guess that's one of the reasons Andrea asked me to write "Dear Heart" even though a whole lot of other girls, including Tessa Ramsey, wanted to do it. I take everything I do very seriously, and Andrea knows I'd never intentionally betray someone's trust.

News travels fast in a small town like Wellbie, especially bad news. Before the end of the day (Thank God! It was Friday), rumors had begun flying around school about Mr. Karch's unexplained absence. It was his first, someone said, in fifteen years of teaching. When TV crews pulled into the parking lot around dismissal time, everybody knew something was up, although nobody knew for sure exactly what.

By the time I'd gotten home from school that afternoon, even my older brother Dave, who's a junior at Wellbie High, had heard ten different rumors about Mr. Karch.

"Hey, sis," Dave greeted me from the couch as I walked into the living room munching on an apple. "Guess there was big news at school today, huh? I heard old Gaylord Karch got canned for lying or something."

"He was suspended," I corrected.

"Fired. Suspended. What's the diff?" Dave said. "It couldn't have happened to a nicer guy. Boy, was he ever strict! I had him back in ninth grade!" He chuckled, put his feet up on the coffee table and began leafing through the latest issue of *Rolling Stone*.

My brother Dave has big dreams of becoming a rock 'n' roll star. He's the lead singer and guitarist in a small band he'd started, called "Slippery Slop." Lately, he's been into some weird kind of music called "garbage punk." Dad, who doesn't have many interests outside his dental practice, hates Dave's music. He calls it "an example of tooth decay of the mind." Mom, who's head of the public relations department at Wellbie Cookies, takes a more tolerant view. She was even sort of proud when Dave's first demo tape, "Mouse for Lunch," became an overnight success in town and rose to the top of the charts of our local radio station.

"Dave," I asked, "what did you mean when you

said Gaylord got fired for lying? That was one of the stories I heard going around school too."

"Oh, I don't know," Dave said. "It was just something somebody mentioned—you know, like he lied to get his job when he first came here." Dave looked up over the top of his magazine. "I mean, can you believe it? All these years, and they're only finding that out now? Hey, are there any more apples left in the fridge?"

The whole story finally came out on the six o'clock news.

Mom was great. After I told her everything about my disaster of a morning, including the big lecture Mr. Buxton had given me, she quickly agreed to make an exception to her usual rules and allow us to eat dinner in front of the tube.

The minute the news came on, I pushed my plate aside and grabbed a pad and pencil to take notes. I wanted to compare the information on TV with the stuff Lance had put in his article.

The lead story was a piece about a huge water main break in the city of Ames, forty miles north of here. Some people had to row to work. Next came a bunch of loud commercials for panty hose, pet deodorant, and Idaho potato chips.

Then Mike Michaelson, the dorky-looking anchorman of Action NewsCenter 6, popped back onto the screen and said with a wry smile, "Well, all's not well in the quiet little town of Wellbie. The Wellbie school system was rocked by scandal today when it was revealed that a veteran math teacher, who was recently nominated for the state's highest teaching award, had allegedly misled school officials for fifteen years about the fact that he'd never gone to college or earned a math degree. Local school board officials announced that Gaylord Karch, chairman of the math department at Wellbie High School, has been suspended from teaching until a final decision can be made in his case. Karch, who refused to speak to reporters today, issued a short written statement, saying, 'I'm completely innocent of all charges.'" The newsman paused. His eyebrows arched slightly. "Deirdre Carruthers, who's been covering the story for NewsCenter 6, has more."

The picture on our set blinked momentarily, and a tall, frizzy-haired brunette appeared on the screen holding a microphone toward two people.

"Holy smokes!" I gasped, jerking forward in my seat. "That's Mr. Buxton, Mom. She's interviewing Mr. Buxton."

"Calm down, Willi," Mom said, "I've got eyes too. I know Larry Buxton when I see him."

"Who's the other person? Do you know?"

"Marybelle Simpson. She's head of the Wellbie school board."

"Geez!" I said. "Mr. Buxton looks pretty fat on TV."

The frizzy-haired reporter leaned toward Mr. Buxton and raised her microphone.

"I'm here at Wellbie High School," she began, "speaking with Larry Buxton, the school's principal. Let me ask you, Larry, is it true the Karch affair actually began on a happy note—when the school received word that Mr. Karch was being considered for a prestigious teaching award?"

"That's absolutely right, Deirdre," Mr. Buxton said. "A month ago, the Iowa State Teachers Association notified us that Mr. Karch had been nominated for a 'MATTY'—its Math Teacher of the Year award."

"And then what happened?"

"Well, naturally the association said it needed to see copies of Mr. Karch's records first. We checked Mr. Karch's file and found everything in there except the records of his college education, which were missing. So the school tried to contact his college and get new records sent. But it quickly discovered that the college Mr. Karch claims he graduated from—Witherspoon College—had burned to the ground about fifteen years ago, around the time Mr. Karch had been hired."

"Ah-hah!" the reporter exclaimed. "I suspect that raised a few eyebrows."

"Yes, it did, Deirdre," Mr. Buxton added, "particularly when we learned that all of Witherspoon's *records* had been destroyed in the fire, too."

Deirdre Carruthers whirled around abruptly to face Marybelle Simpson—so abruptly, in fact, that the frumpy little woman had to jump back to avoid getting hit by the microphone.

"Do you want to pick up the story from there, Mrs. Simpson?" the reporter asked.

"Sure. Well, as president of the school board, I

formed a special committee to study the matter and make recommendations."

"And what did your committee recommend?"

Gripping her needlepoint handbag tightly, Mrs. Simpson said, "Well, Deirdre, we thought it would be best if Mr. Karch didn't continue teaching while his truthfulness was in doubt. Frankly, we were worried about the possible bad influence on the children. We also thought that a temporary suspension might give him the time needed to prove his innocence."

The tall reporter suddenly thrust her microphone back into Mr. Buxton's face and said, "Maybe you could tell us what the school's next step is, Larry—"

"No, I'm sorry I can't comment on that, except to say that our Parent Teacher Association will also be forming a special committee to study the matter, and that we intend to do what's fair and right."

At that point, I stopped taking notes. The reporter was about to give her wrap-up.

"And so there you have it," she said, "the strange story from Wellbie on the Gaylord Karch suspension. I'm Deirdre Carruthers, reporting for Action NewsCenter 6."

Dad clicked off the television with the remote control. Mom wandered over, collecting empty dinner plates (everyone's except mine), and fixed her eyes on my pad.

"Well, did you get anything useful?" she asked.

"Maybe," I said. "There's some, but not a whole lot, of overlap between Lance's article and what

31

really happened. I've got to talk with him next week and straighten things out."

"Good," Mom said. "Now finish your meal."

My food was cold, so I took it back to the kitchen, reheated it in the microwave, and ate it standing up, over the sink. When I returned to fetch my notes, Dad and Dave (who don't normally see eye to eye on much) were agreeing that things looked pretty bad for Gaylord Karch.

"I don't think he deserves to be fired," Dad was saying, "but he deserves to be punished. He shouldn't have lied about his education. Those things always come back to haunt you."

"What makes you so sure he lied, Dad?" I asked, perching on the soft arm of the couch. "Mr. Karch said he didn't do it."

"I can always spot shifty people by their teeth," Dad said. "Mr. Karch has definitely got suspicious-looking teeth." Dad paused as if recalling the shape of Mr. Karch's bicuspids. "What about you, Willi? Do you believe him?"

"I don't know," I said. "Mr. Karch may be many things—and sometimes he makes me so angry I could almost kill him—but I don't think he's a liar."

Dave let out a loud guffaw—one of his mocking laughs that always made me feel about two inches tall.

"What's so funny?" I said.

"You," he said. "You're so gullible. I mean, if Karch was telling the truth, there'd be some documents proving it. But there aren't. You want to know why? Gaylord made everything up. He never went to Witherspoon. He never graduated college. He never got a math degree."

"Okay, Mr. Wise Guy. Then how'd he get hired in the first place? Somebody must have seen his records."

"Easy. He knew Whitherspoon burned down. So he got some phony documents made up—you know, phony grades and a phony diploma. You read about that sort of stuff happening all the time. Face it, Willi. Karch is guilty. He's just guilty."

I was surprised to find myself getting angry. Maybe a bit of Jennifer was rubbing off on me. She always fights for the underdog, and Karch was sure an underdog here.

"You're just saying that," I sputtered, "because you don't like Mr. Karch—because he gave you a D on your report card."

"I don't like him," Dave shot back, "because he ran our class like a total dictator—just like he runs every other class he teaches, including yours."

"Look, I don't like his personality much, either," I said. "But you've got to admit, he's a good math teacher. You went from a D to a B+, didn't you?"

Dave shrugged. "So what? He forced me to. He was on my case all the time."

"Just my point. You were goofing off and he made you stop. One way or another, Mr. Karch makes you learn. Disliking him is no reason for judging him." I suddenly remembered a point I'd wanted to make before. "Besides, if there were all those false documents in his files, where are they now?"

Dave sat up. He had a blank look on his face and didn't say anything.

I glanced at Dad, who'd been totally silent during the whole argument. Now, he picked himself up off the couch and headed for his study, which was off the living room.

"You know, Dave," he said, pausing at the doorway and looking back briefly, "Willi's got an interesting point there, a very interesting point. There may be more to this than meets the eye. I think I'm going to keep an open mind about all this."

At 7:30 PM, promptly, the phone rang. I knew it must be Jennifer.

"I'll get it," I cried, bounding up the stairs two at a time. I made it to the hall phone in three rings and panted a breathless "hello" into the receiver. Jennifer's familiar voice greeted me.

"Hold on a second, Jen," I said as I dragged the phone, on its extra-long extension cord, into my bedroom and closed the door behind me. "Now I'm ready."

"Okay," said Jennifer. "Now tell me everything that happened in Bossy Buxton's office."

So I told her everything, from beginning to end, leaving out no detail.

"Whew!" Jennifer exclaimed after I'd finished. "What a weird coincidence. Do you think Lance knew that Mr. Karch was going to be suspended?"

I tugged on the phone line to get more slack to move around. "Lance swears he made the whole thing up."

"If that's so," Jennifer said, "he ought to go into fortune telling. I'd hire him. He's got an amazing imagination."

"I know. But even if he didn't make it up, I think Mr. Buxton was overracting. There were really only two things in the article that were close to being accurate: the part about Mr. Karch's job being in jeopardy, and the part about his college records."

"Those aren't minor things," Jennifer said.

"Maybe. Maybe not," I said. "But Lance has made up wilder things in the past. And when I saw him this morning on the detention bench, he just didn't look like someone who was covering something up. You've always told me to trust my gut reaction, right?"

"Sure."

"Well, my gut tells me that Lance is telling the truth."

Jennifer paused. "Well, what about Gaylord? Do you think he's a fraud?"

"I don't know," I said. "Everybody seems to be ganging up on him without waiting to hear the evidence."

"I know," said Jennifer. "I got a charge from Lance's article because I was angry with Gaylord about the Math Bee. But then, tonight, when I watched the news with Dad and Duke—"

"Your dad's home?" I interrupted. It was a rarity for Tom Barnes, Jennifer's father, to be in town. He's a computer expert who travels a lot for his job. Jennifer's mother and father are divorced, and her mom now lives in New York. I don't think Jennifer's seen her in years. She never talks about her. So Jennifer lives with her grandfather "Duke," a lovable, eccentric millionaire who collects and trades junk for a hobby.

"Dad got in a few days ago from Dallas," Jennifer said. "I'm so excited. I'm going to have him to myself for two whole weeks, until the seventeenth—St. Patrick's Day."

"That's great," I said, wandering over to my dresser and gazing at the valentine Robbie had given me for Valentine's Day. I sighed, remembering how much fun Robbie and I, and Jennifer and Jim, had had double-dating at the Valentine's Day Dance. Unfortunately, Robbie was in the middle of wrestling season now, and that meant I would hardly see him for a couple of months.

"Anyway," said Jennifer, returning to the subject of Mr. Karch, "after I'd seen the news on TV, I began to feel ashamed about how happy I'd been that he'd been roasted by Lance."

"Yeah," I said. "Even Mr. Karch deserves a fair shake."

"Much as I hate to admit it," Jennifer said, "you're absolutely right—fairness is what this country's about."

Just then, Dave picked up the phone downstairs.

"Hey, why is it that every time I get on the horn to make a call, you girls are gabbing?" he griped.

"Just cool it, Dave," I said.

"I'm not getting off till you guys hang up," he snapped.

36

"Hey, time out—both of you!" cried Jennifer. Then she said, "Look, Willi, I don't want to start World War III in your family. I'd better go. But how about coming over for dinner tomorrow night? We'll get some Chinese take-out from Ming's."

"Sounds great," I said. "But this time let's remember to ask for fortune cookies. They forgot to throw them in the bag the last time."

"Okay. See you tomorrow." Jennifer hung up.

Chapter 4

Late Saturday afternoon I was rereading Lance's column on my bed, when I heard a scratching noise at my second-floor window. At first I thought it was just the rustling of tree branches against the side of the house, so I didn't pay it much attention. Then I heard a tap on the window. There was Jennifer, teetering on the edge of a long branch outside my window—fifteen feet up in the air! Somehow she'd managed to climb the tall maple in the front yard, make her way out the limb outside my bedroom window, lean over, and tap on the glass. I ran over to the window and threw it open.

"Jennifer!" I cried. "Are you crazy! What do you think you're doing?"

"Geronimo!" she yelled, diving head first into my bedroom.

I screamed and covered my eyes. Then I peeked through my fingers.

The instant her hands hit the floor, she tucked her knees up to her chest, rolled forward, and executed a perfect somersault, coming to rest in the center of my rug.

"Not bad for the first try!" she said. "A perfect bull's-eye."

Seconds later, Mom and Dad came pelting upstairs and burst into my room.

"Doesn't anybody knock around here?" I said. "Why can't people just enter my room the normal way?"

"I heard a loud thump. What was that noise?" Dad asked worriedly.

"Jennifer Barnes!" Mom said. "Where did you come from? I didn't see you come in."

"Uh, I only dropped in a moment ago, Mrs. Stevens," Jennifer said, throwing me a wink.

"I guess you've come by to get Willi for dinner," Mom said.

"Yes. Duke's waiting out front in the Jeep with the motor running."

"Please give my regards to your grandfather, honey," Mom said. "It was very nice of him to invite Willi along."

"Sure. He thinks Willi's great," said Jennifer.

Jennifer and I took the stairs down instead of the tree. Two minutes later, we were climbing into the backseat of the Jeep. Behind the steering wheel sat Duke, a short, stockily built man with white hair and a big moustache. He was wearing a battered leather jacket, a long yellow silk scarf, and black hightop sneakers.

"Ready, girls?" he asked. With a loud backfire that shook the windows in the neighborhood, the car roared off.

We picked up our steaming Chinese food at

Ming's while Duke waited outside. Then Jennifer and I piled back into the Jeep, and we all sang rock 'n' roll oldies as we rode on to the largest and prettiest Victorian house in town.

I'd been to Jennifer's house so many times that I wasn't shocked by what I saw when I walked into her living room. In fact, I knew it was a good day when you could even *find* the living room.

Today, the living room was pretty bad. Duke Barnes, retired paperclip king of North America, self-made millionaire, and more recently, creator of the International Junk-of-the-Month Club, had turned the room into a temporary junk warehouse.

Boxes labeled "PILLOW FLUFFERS—DEFECTIVE" were on the sofa. The floor was taken up by piles of inflatable rafts, butter molds (whatever those are), candle snuffers, and slightly used Veg-O-Matics.

"Where's Wilkins?" I asked Jennifer. Wilkins is the Barnes's Australian butler. He's the one who cleans up after Duke and usually keeps the place spotless. I knew that Wilkins would never have allowed Duke's junk to lie around like that.

"Wilkins?" replied Jennifer. "Oh, Duke gave him a month off to visit his mother in Australia."

"And what Wilkins doesn't know won't hurt him," Duke said, smiling at me.

We picked our way through the living room to the dining room. I sat down across from Jennifer. She handed me a white carton filled with egg foo yung while she dove into a dish of chicken with walnuts.

41

All through dinner we talked about our favorite soap opera, *Daylives, Nightlights*. I, for one, was real happy to be talking about something other than Gaylord Karch.

The three of us passed cartons around until I was totally stuffed. "I won't be able to eat another thing for a whole week," I said.

Duke got up to take his plate into the kitchen. "But you're still growing," he said, smiling. "Are you sure you had enough?"

"Oh, boy, did I," I groaned. "Thanks, Duke. It was great."

"Good. Well, you guys know where to find me. I'll be watching the cricket finals on the tube. Willi, just let me know when you're ready to go home."

"Okay, Duke. Thanks." I looked at Jennifer. "Maybe I should just lie down somewhere, like a beached whale."

Jennifer grinned. "Can you manage just one fortune cookie?"

"Well, I guess one can't hurt," I said. I took one, cracked it open, and slipped out my fortune: "'Confucius say: the road to knowledge begins with the turn of a single page.'" I shrugged. "I *would* get one about homework."

Jennifer was reading hers. Suddenly, her eyes widened.

"I'm not superstitious or anything," she said, "but this is ridiculous."

I put my fortune down. "What are you talking about?"

"Here, look at this," Jennifer said, handing me her slip of paper.

I stared at the tiny print. It read: "BEWARE. TROUBLE LIES AHEAD FOR YOUR FAMILY."

I slid the paper back to her across the table.

"That's a creepy one, all right," I said. "But, you're not letting this get to you, are you? You just got a dumb fortune, that's all."

"Would you believe twice in a row?" Jennifer said, giving a nervous toss of her long black hair.

"What do you mean?" I asked.

"I got this exact same fortune twice in two weeks. Once when we had the glop suey special in school and once here. Is that weird or what?"

"It's just a coincidence," I said. "Weird things like that do happen, you know. That's why they're called coincidences."

"Have you ever gotten the same fortune twice in a row?"

I shook my head.

"See?" Jennifer said. "I'm not acting totally crazy. You've got to admit it's spooky."

I studied my friend's face closely. I knew it almost as well as my own. I could sense that Jennifer was keeping something back.

"Jennifer," I began slowly. "What's wrong? Is there something you're not telling me?"

Jennifer played with her chopsticks absently. "Maybe there is," she said. "It's so awful, I've been trying not to think about it."

"What's going on?" I asked, alarmed.

Jennifer sighed. "I guess I should start at the

beginning." She put her chopsticks down. "I already told you my dad's in town, right?"

"Yes," I said. "I wondered where he was tonight. I wanted to say hi." I hadn't seen Mr. Barnes in a couple months, but I could picture him easily in my mind. He's my favorite of all my friends' fathers. Plus, he's definitely one of the handsomest men in Wellbie—which explains why Jennifer is so beautiful.

"If I tell you where he is tonight, you'll die," said Jennifer.

"Try me," I said. "I'm braced." This sounded serious.

"He's at the movies," said Jennifer.

"So?" I said. "Is that a crime?" I breathed a sigh of relief.

"He's at the movies with *Tessa's mother*."

"WHAT?" I shrieked, jumping out of my seat.

"You heard me," said Jennifer. "Now do you see why the fortunes freaked me out? My dad has been *dating* Leona Ramsey!"

I gasped. "Why didn't you tell me? How could this happen?"

Jennifer took a deep breath. "I didn't say anything because I couldn't believe it was serious. It all started when Dad and I were shopping at the Piggly Wiggly. We were in the dairy section. He bent over to get a blueberry yogurt and banged right into this woman who was reaching for some pineapple cottage cheese. It was Leona, dressed to kill, as usual. I saw their eyes meet. Then Leona dropped her pineapple cottage cheese on the floor.

44

Dad picked it up for her, and she fell all over herself thanking him."

"Gross!" I exclaimed.

"Tessa was with her, and she saw the whole thing, too. She looked just as disgusted as I was."

"For once, you agreed on something," I said.

"Anyhow, one thing led to another, and by the time we were at the check-out counter, Dad and Leona were exchanging phone numbers. Tessa and I could only watch helplessly."

"This is unbelievable," I said, shaking my head.

"Believe it. I saw it happen."

"But your dad knows how you feel about Tessa."

"No, he doesn't. He's never here long enough to know much about my life, or who I hate." I had never heard Jennifer talk about her dad this way.

"Look, Jennifer, I bet that whatever's going on, nothing will come of it."

"Don't be so sure," she said glumly. "He's divorced, she's divorced. They're both pretty good looking. Need I say more? Oh, I'm so freaked out, Willi. I flunked a biology quiz on Wednesday. I burnt my breakfast yesterday. What if they actually fall in love? Tessa—Tessa could become my stepsister!"

I sat there and tried to absorb the enormity of this tragedy. It was worse than the episode of *Daylives, Nightlights* where Rachel found out that her husband Frank had married three other women during his bout with amnesia after the car accident.

"Well, there's always my house," I said weakly.

"My parents will adopt you." It was a dumb joke that didn't get a laugh.

"You've got to help me figure out what to do, Willi. I'm a total wreck."

"You know I'll help, Jennifer," I said. "Any way I can. We can't let this happen—and we won't."

Later the three of us all piled back into Duke's Jeep and headed for my house.

At the door, Jennifer and I had a hurried conversation.

"Don't worry about you know what," I said. "We'll think of something."

"I'm counting on you, Willi. I'm at my wits' end," she whispered to me.

An hour later, I lay on my bed, gazing up at the ceiling and thinking. Jennifer was freaking out. It just didn't compute. Of all my friends, Jennifer is the strongest, the coolest, the most resourceful—the only one I truly look up to. I always imagine her as fourteen going on seventeen. I'm always the one to have Jennifer around to help me over the rough spots in my life. It was strange and scary to suddenly hear Jennifer asking for *my* help. Deep down inside of me, I wondered if I had what it took to be Jennifer's Jennifer.

Chapter 5

When Monday rolled around, it soon became clear that Tessa was up to her old tricks again.

I got off the school bus that morning, as usual, and walked around to the back of the school toward the shed, where Jennifer and I often meet before homeroom. The shed is a small wooden building—a miniature house, really—with a little porch and a cute two-seater bench attached to the railing. From the porch bench, you can see the rolling Wellbie hillside and—just barely—the twin turrets of Jennifer's house rising above the trees on the far side of the golf course. Since Jennifer generally walks to school, cutting across the sixteenth hole, the shed makes an ideal halfway meeting place for us.

Nobody from the golf course ever seemed to mind that two girls would meet on the porch for ten minutes or so on sunny, pleasant mornings.

Nobody, that is, until today.

As I traipsed down the hill, picking up clumps of burrs on my jacket, I saw Jennifer standing on the porch, her hands on her hips, talking—no, arguing, was more like it—with a tall, thin figure dressed in gray coveralls and a down vest. I broke into a run and reached the shed in nothing flat, stumbling a bit as I leaped onto the porch. At my thudding arrival, the bickering stopped. Jennifer turned, and the tall, thin figure stepped out of the shadowy doorway so that I could see his face.

Turk Guffey!

Jennifer came over to me, looking depressed, and jerked a thumb over her shoulder in the maintenance man's direction.

"Turk says we can't meet here anymore. The shed's off limits."

"What?" I exclaimed. "Who says we can't?"

Turk put his hands up like a traffic cop. "Look, all I know is somebody called the golf course yesterday and said she saw some girls throwing rocks at the shed before school. The golf course called the school, and Mr. Buxton told me to get down here and keep all the kids away."

"She?" Jennifer asked, her eyes narrowing.

"Right. It was some woman." Turk fidgeted uncomfortably with the tool pouch he wore on his belt. "Listen," he said, "I'm sure she wasn't talking about you two, but it ain't my business to question Mr. Buxton. I'm just trying to do my job here."

We turned to leave the shed and trudge back up the hill to homeroom. Turk walked behind us, and said, "Say, you girls are in Emma's math class, aren't you?"

"Uh-huh," I said, not feeling much like chatting with him right then about his daughter.

"I'll bet you're happy about what happened to

48

Gaylord Karch, huh? That guy's been horrible to Emma."

"Mr. Karch treats everybody equally," said Jennifer. "Mean."

"I sure hope he gets what's coming to him," Turk said angrily.

I knew how much Emma suffered in Karch's class, and I felt bad for her father. But I was also starting to feel uncomfortable about bad-mouthing Karch all the time. It seemed like kicking a guy when he was down.

It was time to get to homeroom. We were pretty bummed out as we walked into the language arts building and stopped off at my locker. Jennifer leaned one shoulder against the locker next to mine.

"You know, I think the two of us have probably set some kind of new world's record for bad luck," she said.

"Yeah," I agreed with a bitter laugh. "First I get in trouble with Mr. Buxton, then your dad goes temporarily insane, and now we get bumped from our favorite place."

I slammed my locker closed, and Jennifer and I made our way to Mademoiselle Paulette's class for homeroom. I wondered whether our bad luck was fate. Or maybe fate had had a push in the right direction.

Later in gym class, Jennifer and I found out who was behind our eviction from the shed.

It was an uncommonly warm morning for late winter, and the air was filled with the heavenly scent of Vanilla Supreme Cookies being baked a few miles down the road at the Wellbie Cookie Company. Miss LaRue, our gym teacher, had taken the class outside for a grueling two-mile run ("It'll be great for your tummies and thighs, girls!") up and down the hills around the playing fields behind the school. We'd started out as a group of about twenty-five girls all bunched together in a tight formation. By the time the first runner had crossed the finish line, the pack had gotten stretched out into a line over fifty yards long. As usual, I'd slipped back toward the rear, and was huffing and puffing to keep up. Jennifer, who could have easily come in first, was jogging slowly alongside me, offering words of encouragement to help me take my mind off my bursting lungs.

My legs got heavier and heavier. Finally, I knew my body couldn't hold out one second longer, and even though the finish line was less than a quarter of a mile ahead, I gasped to Jennifer that I had to drop out and walk the rest of the way. Jennifer slowed down and began to walk, too. I draped one arm over her neck for support while I struggled to catch my breath.

Suddenly, I looked up and saw Tessa jogging back in our direction. She was flanked by two members of her clique, Fran Gerber and Erica Moss. They stopped a few yards ahead of us and planted themselves squarely in our path.

Jennifer and I halted. I slipped my arm from Jennifer's shoulder and stood up straight. Sweat was dripping from my forehead.

Tessa drew herself up, too, and with a well-practiced motion, gave a flip of her long red hair.

The gesture had a mixture of vanity and arrogance to it. In spite of myself, I had to admit she made a pretty picture. She was wearing a colorful designer gym suit that set off her striking green eyes.

"What do you want, Tessa?" Jennifer asked curtly.

A thin smile broke on Tessa's face. "My, my, Jennifer. Is that any way to greet a friend? I just wanted to offer my sympathies. I heard you girls got kicked out of the shed this morning. What an awful thing to happen."

Tessa shot a quick glance at Fran and Erica, who couldn't restrain themselves from snickering.

Jennifer said, "Where did you hear that?"

"Oh, I don't know," Tessa said. "These things get around quickly. You just hear them."

"Of course, *you* wouldn't have had anything to do with it, would you?" Jennifer continued.

Tessa batted her eyelashes, feigning an air of injured innocence. "Me? Do you think I'd do something like that?"

"Why, you—" I started.

"Cool it, Willi," Jennifer said. "That's not going to solve anything."

"But—she could've gotten us expelled or something."

Miss LaRue blew her whistle from the finish line. "Jennifer, Willi, Tessa—all you girls!" she hollered. "Hurry up!"

"We're coming, Miss LaRue!" Tessa shouted back.

"Cut the act and get to the point, Tessa," Jennifer said.

51

A veil dropped from Tessa's face.

"Okay. I don't know what your dad is trying to pull, but I don't like it. You tell him to keep away from my mom. Things will start going much easier for you if he does."

Jennifer exploded. "What *my* dad's pulling?" she exclaimed. "*Your* mom is the one who's causing all the trouble."

"Oh, yeah?" Tessa snapped. "Who's been asking her out?"

"Who's been falling all over herself saying yes?"

Miss LaRue blew her whistle again.

"I didn't say next year, girls," she yelled through her cupped hands. "I said NOW!"

Fran Gerber, the spineless wonder, began to get nervous. She tugged at Tessa's arm and whined, "C'mon, Tessa. Let's get back. I don't want to get in trouble."

"Okay," said Tessa, making a move to go. "I've said everything I needed to say."

"Wait a minute, Tessa," I said, seizing the opportunity to get a word in edgewise. "You know, I always thought you took after your mom. Now I know I was wrong. At least your mom can manage to snag a cute guy. Too bad you can't."

Tessa's face turned a bright red that matched the color of her hair. She knew I meant Robbie. Glaring at me with silent rage, she and her two friends sprinted off to rejoin the class.

Jennifer and I followed, but at a good distance behind.

Chapter 6

Mr. Buxton had said we would be getting a teacher to fill in for Mr. Karch pretty soon, but I didn't know how hard up he was for substitutes until I walked into my seventh-period math class. Miss LaRue was sitting behind Mr. Karch's desk in her baby-blue warmup suit. *She couldn't be teaching us,* I thought. The only math she knew was counting from one to ten.

"Attention! Attention, boys and girls!" Miss LaRue said in a perky voice. "I have a very important announcement to make. I'm taking over your class, temporarily, for Mr. Karch, who—I'm sure you know by now—won't be able to be with us for the next few weeks."

A loud cheer went up from the class.

"Quiet. Let's have it quiet in here," she ordered.

When the noise died down, she continued: "Now, I know we're going to have lots of fun learning about—" She looked down at Mr. Karch's lesson plans. ". . . Ratios and purportions."

"Proportions," called out Jim Ellis.

"Oh, yes. That's right," said Miss LaRue. "Before

we begin, it would be nice if we all did some deep breathing exercises to clear out all the cobwebs from our brains."

Miss LaRue pushed her chair back and bounced to her feet.

"Everybody up now!" she said. "Stand by your seats."

There was a squeaking of chairs and a shuffling of feet as everybody stood up.

"Good," she said. "Now let your arms just rise up and float in space. Breathe deeply. Imagine you're a butterfly settling on a flower. Everybody think like a butterfly."

A lot of puzzled looks went flying around the room.

Bucky Armbruster raised his hand with a question. "What kind of butterfly do you mean?"

"I beg your pardon?" asked Miss LaRue.

"Well, there are monarchs, admirals, zebras, hairstreaks, painted ladies. They all behave differently."

Miss LaRue was nonplussed. To the sweet but literal-minded Bucky, the whole world centers around farming, and the plants, animals, and insects associated with it. In fact, the closest he had come to saying "I love you" to Jennifer last year was to name his prize heifer's newborn calf after her: Jennifer Julep.

"Uh, why don't you try being a monarch, Bucky?" Miss LaRue responded. "They have big wings, don't they?"

"Real big, and they can fly long distances."

"That's our butterfly, then!" Miss LaRue declared. "Listen up, class," she announced. "I want you each to think like a *monarch* butterfly."

"Oh, brother," Jennifer mumbled under her breath. "Mr. Karch was impossible, but Miss LaRue's a total disaster."

I nodded in agreement.

Two dozen pairs of arms floated up all over the classroom.

For ten minutes, I breathed deeply and tried to think like a monarch butterfly. But the only thought that came to my mind was that if this was the way Miss LaRue was going to teach algebra, I was going to have to be in high school for the rest of my life.

At 3:05 PM, as Jennifer and I were leaving Miss Larue's "better math through better breathing" class, Andrea Wellbie was waiting outside the door for me. She was dressed in one of her hand-tailored tweedy outfits and was carrying a thin leather briefcase.

"Pardon me, Jennifer," Andrea said as she pulled me aside. "I've got to talk to Willi about some newspaper business."

Jennifer stiffened a little. I'd seen that reaction before—like when I'd had to cancel our regular dates to watch *Daylives, Nightlights* because I was frantically trying to write "Dear Heart" to meet my weekly deadline. Jennifer knew how much my job on *The Real McCoy* meant to me, and she was my biggest booster when it came to giving me confidence in my writing and editing abilities. But she also clearly resented Andrea's power over me and was jealous of the amount of time the newspaper took away from our friendship.

"Is this going to be short, Andrea?" Jennifer asked. "Or should I not bother waiting?"

Andrea winced slightly. I knew she didn't want to say anything that might set Jennifer off—especially about the newspaper. Andrea and I had really had our hands full last fall when Jennifer had launched her campaign to ban "Dear Heart." We never wanted to go through something like that again.

Andrea tried diplomacy. She put her hand lightly on Jennifer's shoulder and said tactfully, "I'm sorry, Jennifer, but something really important has come up. I've got to hold a staff meeting with Willi and Lance at *The Real McCoy* office."

Jennifer's eyes narrowed. "Willi's not in any more trouble, is she?" she asked suspiciously.

Andrea shook her head. "Believe me," she said, "this meeting has only one purpose: to find a way that Willi, Lance, and I can get back into Mr. Buxton's good graces."

Then Andrea turned to me and said, "Willi, I forgot to ask if you can stay late today. If you need a ride later, my chauffeur can drive you home."

"No, that's okay," I said. "If the meeting doesn't last too long, I can catch the late bus."

"Good. Then I'll see you at the newspaper office in fifteen minutes. Lance will meet us there."

Andrea ducked into the math room to say hi to

Tessa, who was busy buttering up Miss LaRue, and Jennifer and I headed out of the building.

"I guess I was pretty touchy with Andrea," Jennifer said apologetically. "I didn't mean to embarrass you."

"You didn't," I replied. "I understand. I've punked out on you a lot because of her."

Jennifer sighed. "Did you ever feel like you just weren't yourself? Like you were somebody else?"

"Are you kidding?" I said. "I get that feeling practically every morning. I wake up and ask myself, who am I going to be today? The klutz? The failed dieter? The zit-faced wonder? Some day I'd just like to wake up and be my true self—you know, Marilyn Monroe."

Jennifer smiled. "I love you, Willi. You always make me laugh—even when I'm not feeling like it."

"What's wrong, Jennifer? You really sound down. Is it your dad and Leona?"

"Yeah. It's got me totally bummed out. I was really hoping, this time around, to get some quality time with Dad. He *promised* me. He's been promising me that for months. And now it's 'Sorry, honey, I've got to go out tonight,' or 'Maybe tomorrow, Jennifer, I'm taking Leona to a concert.'"

Jennifer's eyes suddenly looked teary. It was such a shock (I'd never seen her cry about anything), I almost turned away.

"You okay?" I asked, taking her arm.

"Yeah," she said, regaining her composure. "I'm all right."

"Just look at it this way," I said, trying to be optimistic. "The worst that can happen is that they see each other for two weeks, and then it's over. Am I right?"

"Wrong. The worst is that they fall in love and I get Tessa the Terrible for a *stepsister*."

"You think they might actually fall in love if they keep seeing each other for two more weeks?"

"Two weeks can be an eternity. Remember what happened to Ernie, Maxine's father, in *Daylives, Nightlights*? He fell in love with Roberta the dentist after just three visits to her office."

I gulped, remembering the episodes. Roberta had really gotten her dental tools into Ernie. Those episodes were the only ones I'd ever gotten my dad to watch with me.

"It's even starting to affect my social life," Jennifer continued. "Jim called yesterday and asked me to go to the movies with him. But I told him no—I wanted to keep my afternoon open just in case Dad decided to hang out with me. You know what happened? Leona called, and Dad wound up going over to her house to put up some shelves in her kitchen. He didn't come back until after dinnertime."

We were now outside the administration building, where the newspaper office was located.

"Look, Jen," I said. "I'm sorry, but I gotta go. Don't let this get you down too much. In a couple of weeks this is all going to seem a big joke."

Jennifer managed a weak smile and gave me a

hug. Then she turned and walked off slowly toward the buses, her shoulders hunched over.

The editorial office of *The Real McCoy* is a small, airless room sandwiched between the *Wellbie World* yearbook office and the office of the Wellbie chapter of the Future Farmers of America. Whenever we have full staff meetings and have to seat a dozen kids (plus Mr. Purdy) around the work table, it gets pretty cramped in there. But this afternoon, with just Andrea, Lance, and me in the office, there was plenty of room to spare.

"Okay, Lance," Andrea said after she'd called the meeting to order. "I want to talk about what happened on Friday. Willi and I have heard what Mr. Buxton had to say. Now, I want to hear it from your lips." She held up the disputed newspaper issue. "Did you or did you not make up that story on Mr. Karch?"

"I'm real sorry, Andrea," Lance began. "I had no idea we'd get into such hot water. But you gotta believe me. Mr. Buxton jumped to the wrong conclusion. My article's fiction."

Andrea pressed on with her questioning. "Mr. Buxton thinks you got your idea from somebody on the school board, or that you got hold of some secret school board memo or something."

"C'mon, Andrea," the Twerp replied defensively. "I don't know anybody on the school board. I don't even know what the school board *does*. I swear I didn't know Mr. Karch was being investigated. It was just a weird coincidence."

There were those words again: "weird coincidence." No matter where I turned, I couldn't seem to escape them. Weird coincidences seemed to be going on around Wellbie like a bad cold.

"Go on. I'm listening," Andrea said.

"Look, I know it sounds fishy," he continued. "But the idea just came to me while I was sitting in my doctor's office, waiting for my allergy shots. I was bored and didn't have anything to do, so I got out my notebook and wrote the whole story there. I even asked the nurse how to spell 'sniveling.' You can call her up and ask. I'll give you the number."

Lance sneezed and blew his nose. He was oddly proud of the fact that he was allergic to about a hundred different things.

Andrea stared at the Twerp for a long time. "All right, Lance," she said. "I'm giving you the benefit of the doubt. Let's consider the matter closed."

Lance sighed with relief. "Thanks, Andrea," he said. His face brightened. He had the look of an accused man who's just managed to establish his innocence.

At this moment, Andrea decided to drop her bombshell. In front of her was an envelope. "Here," she said, withdrawing the letter inside. "I found this lying on the floor in here around noon. Someone must have shoved it under the door. I want both of you to read it."

The Twerp and I huddled together. I picked up the letter. On a sheet of lined notebook paper was written:

TO THE EDITOR OF *THE REAL MCCOY:*

MR. KARCH IS INNOCENT AND I CAN PROVE
IT. I WILL CONTACT YOU SOON.

A CONCERNED STUDENT

"Holy smokes!" said Lance. "What do you make
of it?"

"I don't know," I said, flabbergasted. "It could be
a prank. It could be the truth. I just don't know."

We both sat there with our mouths hanging
open, just gaping at each other, and at Andrea.

"I smell a real big news story," said Lance, his
eyes starting to glow. "Everybody thinks Mr. Karch
is guilty. If we can prove he's not, we could
outscoop everybody."

"That's what I think," said Andrea excitedly. "It
could—"

A loud knock on the door interrupted her
thought. Andrea opened the door, and there stood
Mr. Buxton!

"Oh, uh, hello Mr. Buxton," Andrea said, fum-
bling for words. "How are you?"

"Fine," Mr. Buxton said in a flat voice. "I was
walking by and I heard some talking in here. I
thought I'd just pop in and see what was going on."
He stepped inside the door. I quickly grabbed the
envelope and letter and stuffed them into my
knapsack. "Discussing next week's issue, perhaps?"
Mr. Buxton asked.

Andrea thought fast. "Er—yes," she said, "but
we're done. We're locking up now. Willi and the
Twerp—I mean, Lance—have to catch the late

61

bus." Andrea threw me and Lance a wink that Mr. Buxton couldn't see.

Picking up on her cue, Lance and I gathered our things and made a hasty departure. As I passed by Andrea, she said to me, "Call me at home tonight, Willi, so we can tie up some of the loose ends about that student's letter, okay?"

I nodded.

This was one letter, I knew, that had to be handled ultra carefully—or we could wind up in an even deeper mess than we were already.

Chapter 7

I phoned Andrea from my bedroom after dinner. I started to ask her about the strange letter we'd gotten, but she cut me short.

"Hold it, Willi!" she said. "I'm down in the library right now *with Daddy and Mother*. I think it would be best if we discussed this problem on my *private* line upstairs. Hang up and I'll call you back."

"Oh," I said. "Your parents are standing right next to you, and you can't talk."

"Right," said Andrea. "So let me go upstairs and call you back in five, okay?"

"Sure," I said, and hung up the phone.

It was actually more like twenty minutes before Andrea finally got back to me. It had probably taken her a good fifteen minutes just to reach the east wing of the Wellbie mansion, where her bedroom is.

"There," Andrea said, after we'd reestablished phone contact. "Now we can talk freely."

"What was the problem?" I asked.

"Oh, it's Daddy and Mother," Andrea replied

gloomily. "I didn't want them to overhear us. They're being so impossible about this whole Karch thing."

"What do you mean?"

"Well, they're really upset with me. Daddy hit the ceiling when he heard I'd gotten bawled out by Mr. Buxton."

"You told him about it?"

"No, Mr. Buxton did, when they bumped into each other at the Racquet Club on Saturday. That made everything worse. Daddy came home just fit to be tied. He sat me down and lectured me about the 'honor of the Wellbies'—how Wellbies have standards to uphold, how Wellbies *never* get into trouble." Andrea sighed. "You know, Willi, I've heard that speech about ten million times. Daddy always forgets to mention about how many times he'd gotten kicked out of private schools before the age of eleven."

"Yeah," I sympathized. "All parents have amazingly short memories when it suits their purposes."

"You can say that again," Andrea said.

I quickly switched the subject back to the issue of the Karch letter.

"Do you think it could be a hoax?" I asked. "I mean, do you think somebody might be trying to get us into deeper trouble?"

"I don't know. That's always a possibility."

"Maybe we should ignore it, then."

"Are you crazy?" exclaimed Andrea. "And miss the scoop of our lives? If we could turn up evidence that Gaylord's innocent, we'd be journalistic heroes. If we could break the story before anybody else, then *The Real McCoy* could really make news—maybe even national news. That would get us out of hot water with Mr. Buxton for sure, and it would show my father once and for all that I'm not irresponsible."

"Well, what's our next move?"

"You know what I think?" Andrea said. "I think *The Real McCoy* is going to set up a secret investigative unit to cover the Karch story. It'll be you and the Twerp. We won't tell Mr. Purdy—the shock might make the rest of his hair fall out. You and Lance will report back to me on your progress. When we get the proof we need, we'll go public with the story. Even Mr. Buxton will thank us when we're done."

"Any ideas where we should begin? What can we do about the note, for instance?"

"Nothing right now," Andrea replied. "We'll just have to sit tight until the person who wrote it contacts us again."

"And in the meantime?"

"I think you and the Twerp should pay a call on Mr. Karch and get his story. If he really did go to that college, he's got to have some stuff lying around that could prove it. All we need is a crumb to go on. But it's got to be a tasty crumb."

I thought that was well put, even for a cookie heiress.

"But what if Gaylord won't talk to us?" I said. "What if he tries to rip Lance in half because of the column he wrote?"

"Hmm," said Andrea, "that's a good point. I never thought of that. I don't know what you'd do then. Just use your head, Willi. You'll figure something out. If you can just make Gaylord understand that you're really trying to help, I'm sure he'll cooperate."

I felt a throbbing in my hand. I looked down and noticed I'd wound the telephone cord too tightly around my finger.

"All right," I said, unraveling the coils and freeing my hand. "I don't know why I'm doing this, but I'll do it."

"Good," said Andrea. "I knew you would. And who knows? If we pull this off, there might be a promotion in it for you. You've been itching to move up from copy manager to investigative reporter, haven't you?"

"Sure," I said. "You know I have."

"Well, here's your chance to prove yourself. But whatever you do, you've got to be careful. Remember, we're going up against popular opinion, so we'll need to gather convincing evidence—much harder stuff than an anonymous message shoved under a door."

"I know," I said. "I hope we can find it."

"Me too," agreed Andrea.

Then we said our goodbyes and hung up.

I called Lance immediately and told him about Andrea's decision. He was incredibly excited about getting a secret investigative assignment, but totally freaked about having to go interview Mr. Karch. I did my best to reassure him. I told him not

66

to worry—that I would try very hard to keep Mr. Karch from killing him. It didn't reduce his fears much.

"I'm making out my will before I go," he said. "I want you to witness it."

Lance paused, his voice cracking with emotion. "Do you think you'd like to have my red baseball cap, Willi?" he asked gravely. "I'd like you to have it—if, you know, anything should happen to me."

"Sure, Twerp, sure," I said, feeling touched by his gesture. "You know I'd treasure it always."

Ten minutes after I'd finished talking with Lance, the phone rang again. It was Andrea.

"Andrea!" I said. "Long time no speak. What's up?"

"Well," she replied slowly, "I suddenly remembered that there was one more important thing I wanted to discuss with you."

"If it's about Lance," I began eagerly, "I just got off the phone with him—"

"This has nothing to do with the Karch story." Andrea took a long, deep breath. "It's about Tessa and Jennifer."

"You mean about what's been going on between Tessa's mom and Jennifer's dad? It's disgusting, isn't it? You'd think they'd have better sense."

"They're acting like children," said Andrea. "It's revolting."

There was an awkward silence. Then Andrea said, "Willi, can I ask you something confidentially— girl to girl? How's Jennifer dealing with all of this?"

"She's upset, naturally," I replied. "What would you expect? How about Tessa?"

Andrea sighed. "She's upset too."

I shifted my position on the bed. There was another long silence, which Andrea broke again.

"You know," she said, "I wish there was something we could do. I mean, I think Tessa and Jennifer are both kind of stressed out. It would be good if we could keep them from taking it out on each other."

"Oh," I said. "So you heard about what happened at the shed?"

"That was an honest mistake!" Andrea said. "Tessa really did see some girls throwing rocks down there."

I decided to hold my tongue. "Okay, forget I said it," I mumbled. I guess I couldn't blame her for sticking up for her best friend. I would have.

Andrea simmered down. "What I was hoping, Willi, was that maybe you and I could sort of watch out for Jennifer and Tessa until Mr. Barnes and Tessa's mother grow out of this thing."

"Sounds fine to me," I said. "Jennifer and Tessa have been battling tooth and nail. If they step up their war, one of them is bound to get hurt."

"Right," said Andrea. "And if it gets any uglier, a lot of *other* people are going to get hurt too—like maybe you and me."

I gave a wry laugh. "Well, at least time's on our side. Mr. Barnes is scheduled to leave town soon on another long business trip."

"You know when?"

"March seventeenth, I think."

"Good. That's less than two weeks away. Hmm . . ." she said. "I'll make you a deal, Willi. I'll promise to keep Tessa out of Jennifer's hair during that time if you'll promise to keep Jennifer out of Tessa's. How's that?"

I thought about it for a minute. "And what happens after March seventeenth?"

"They're both back on their own."

I remembered how I'd promised Jennifer that I'd do anything to find a way to help her get through this mess. Andrea's idea seemed like a good place to start.

"Okay," I said firmly. "You've got a deal."

"Great!" exclaimed Andrea. "That's what I hoped to hear. Bye, Willi," she said. "Let's keep in touch on this."

And so we concluded our third phone conversation of the night.

My ear was just beginning to recover from a sever case of telephone-itis, when the phone rang again.

"I'll get it, Mom!" I screamed through my door. "It's probably Andrea, Part Four."

"Hello," I said.

"It's me, Jennifer."

There was a disturbing quality to Jennifer's voice.

"Jennifer, are you okay?" I asked.

"No," she moaned. "I'm not okay. I just finished screaming into a pillow for an hour. Now I'm standing on my head to try and stay calm. I feel like I'm going to explode."

"Why? What's wrong?"

"Dad."

"Uh-oh. What now?"

"He's going moonlight ice-skating with Tessa's mom tonight."

I gulped. "I can't stand it."

"And that's not all. He's come up with another excuse to see her. Promise you won't laugh."

"I promise."

"He's joined the PTA."

I couldn't help it. I just had to laugh. The thought of Jennifer's dashing, attractive father (who knows so little about our town) joining the boring, straight-laced PTA seemed too ridiculous for words.

"Why did he do that?" I asked. "What's the connection?"

"Well, remember what Mr. Buxton said on TV last week—that the PTA was going to form its own committee to study what to do with Mr. Karch?"

"Uh-huh."

"Well, Leona is on that committee, and she asked Dad to join. So he did. Now they've got an extra reason to meet together."

"Oh brother!" I said. "It's making me sick to my stomach."

I heard a loud thump on her end of the line, like a pair of bare feet hitting the floor.

"If *that* makes you sick," Jennifer said, "this will make you sicker. Guess who's coming over to dinner Thursday night?"

I shuddered. "He didn't!"

"He did. He's invited Leona *and Tessa* over for Duke's Thursday Night Special. Dad wants us to have a 'nice, cozy two-family evening' together. Can you believe it?"

"Omigosh! What a dope!" was all I could say.

"Willi," Jennifer said. "You gotta help me out. I won't be able to get through this meal alone. I might do something I'd regret for the rest of my life. You've got to come, too. Will you?"

I swallowed hard. "Of course, Jennifer. You know I wouldn't miss the Tom and Leona horror hour for all the world."

Chapter 8

On Wednesday morning before school, our mysterious tipster struck again. I went to *The Real McCoy* office to check the "Dear Heart" box for new letters and bumped into Andrea at the door, struggling with the lock. When she finally got her key to work and we went inside, we found that another note had been slipped under the door.

This one read:

> HE'S NOT A BAD PERSON. HE DIDN'T MEAN
> TO DO IT. I DON'T WANT HIM TO BE PUNISHED.
> I'LL LEAVE SOME IMPORTANT INFORMATION IN
> AN ENVELOPE IN THE AUDITORIUM AFTER SCHOOL
> ON THURSDAY.
>
> A CONCERNED STUDENT.

"We'd better call an emergency meeting of the R.M.S.I.U.," Andrea said in a hushed tone.

"The what?" I asked.

"*The Real McCoy* Special Investigative Unit—that's you and Lance. We'll meet here during lunch period."

I got hold of Lance during homeroom and informed him of the new development. When noontime rolled around, the two of us headed over to the newspaper office, our brown paper lunch-bags in hand.

"Well, what do you think?" Andrea asked after Lance and I had settled into our seats and she'd locked the door behind us.

Lance took off his red cap and scratched his head. "Beats me," he said. "This letter's too confusing. I mean, like WHO's not a bad person? WHO didn't mean to do it? Are we talking about Mr. Karch or somebody else?"

I took a bite of my bologna sandwich. "It wouldn't make sense if it was Mr. Karch," I said. "The first letter said that Mr. Karch was innocent. Being innocent and 'not meaning to do it' aren't exactly the same things."

Andrea nodded. "I agree," she said. "It seems to me that this person is talking about someone else."

She opened her briefcase and took out a bag of cookies.

"Try a few," she said, passing the bag around. "Tell me how you like 'em. They're brand new from the Wellbie Test Bakery. They're called Butterscotch Creamies. Daddy thinks they're going to be as popular as Vanilla Supremes."

Lance grabbed a handful. I took two. They smelled great.

"Maybe our letter-writer is protecting somebody." I said, wishing I had a diet soda to wash down the bologna.

74

"Maybe he's protecting *himself*," threw in Lance. "He could be referring to himself as 'he' instead of 'I' just to throw us off the track."

"That's too complicated, Lance," I said. "Why would he—or she—slip us these notes if he didn't want to cooperate?"

"That's right," Andrea said. "It wouldn't make sense." She munched thoughtfully on a Butterscotch Creamie. "If our letter-writer *is* protecting someone, it's probably somebody else—someone who *did* something that has a bearing on the Karch case. That's why I want both of you to stake out the auditorium after school tomorrow. See if you can find out who's been writing these notes. Search the place and find that envelope!"

Later that night as I was writing my "Dear Heart" column for next week's issue, I found it hard to keep my mind on my work. I kept wondering what, if anything, Lance and I would find in the auditorium tomorrow and when, if ever, I'd ever win a promotion from anonymous advice columnist to investigative reporter.

It would have been nice if our stakeout on Thursday had ended successfully, the way they do on all the cop shows on TV. But it was a total bust—at least as far as uncovering the identity of our anonymous letter-writer was concerned. The Wellbie High auditorium is probably the worst place on earth to have to monitor with just two people. It has too many entrances that someone could slip in through or out of unnoticed.

Lance and I tried to watch the auditorium during the day, ducking in there whenever we had a free moment to see if we could catch somebody doing something suspicious. But the only people we surprised were Paul Huffel and Erica Moss, who were making out during third period in the last row. Andrea even got us passes from Mr. Purdy to get Lance and me out of study hall so we could hang out in the auditorium for a whole period. But when we took up our spying positions behind the curtains on the stage, the Twerp had a series of sneezing fits that kept blowing our cover. So we abandoned our positions and decided to search the place for our envelope. But it was nowhere to be found.

All day long, Jennifer moaned and groaned about tonight's dinner party, mentioning to me repeatedly that she "just didn't understand" her dad at all, that he was acting like a "colossal dingbat." She also said she felt like making a nasty scene tonight, but she didn't want to hurt or embarrass her dad.

Yet even though she was deeply preoccupied with her own troubles, she didn't fail to notice how strange *I* was behaving today—dashing off the minute a period had ended (always to the stupid auditorium) without waiting for her or giving her an explanation. When I'd rejoin her at our next class, she'd bombard me with questions about where I had been and what I had been doing. For six periods, I managed to fend her off. Finally, I decided it wasn't fair of me to keep her in the dark any longer. She had enough on her mind as it was without my adding to her problems. So, after math class, as I was preparing to return to the auditorium for the tenth time, I filled her in about the mysterious Karch letters and the newly formed R.M.S.I.U.

As she listened, her eyes widened. "Do you mean somebody framed Mr. Karch?" she asked.

"I don't know," I said. "That's what we're trying to find out."

Jennifer gave my arm a squeeze and said, "Well, if anybody can do it, it's you, Willi."

I also told her the good news—about my possible promotion. Jennifer's face brightened for the first time that day. "All right!" she exclaimed. "That Andrea's not such a dork after all. Except, she shouldn't dangle that job in front of you like a carrot. She ought to just give it to you. That's what I'd do."

"Thanks, Jen," I said. "But you're not Andrea Wellbie. Besides, I really want to earn it. I don't want Andrea to give it to me."

Jennifer shrugged. "You're crazy, but I can see your point."

We stopped at the center of the school grounds, and Jennifer said, "I'd help you look for the envelope, but I've got to go home and clean up for tonight. Can you come over early?"

"Around seven-ish?"

"How about six-thirty?"

"Okay. Six-thirty, on the dot."

"Thanks, Willi. I'm counting on you."

* * *

When I got to the auditorium, Lance was doing a cute little jig on the stage and grinning from ear to ear. He jumped down and ran over, waving a large brown manila envelope in the air.

"It was on the piano," he said, "tucked behind some music."

Written on the front of the envelope were the words: "TO *THE REAL McCOY*."

"Don't just stand there," I said. "Open it."

Lance and I gazed around the auditorium to make sure that nobody else had strolled in. Then he tore open the envelope. I expected to see some documents or papers inside, records that might help us prove Mr. Karch's innocence. I wasn't prepared for what we did find, because it was so peculiar. In that brown envelope was a small, green, odd-shaped piece of fuzzy cardboard that looked like part of a jigsaw puzzle.

The Twerp figured out what it was first. "You know what this is?" he said. "It's a piece from a teacher's blotter."

"Oh, great!" I said sarcastically. "That's just the hard evidence we need." I took the flimsy piece of cardboard and bent it back and forth with my fingers to illustrate my point. "Somebody's playing games with us."

"Wait a minute!" Lance said, poking me in the ribs. "Let me have it."

Lance snatched it out of my hands and flipped it over. On the underside, I could see, were written two words: "MR. BUXTON."

I looked at Lance, and he looked at me. We didn't speak for at least a minute.

"Do you think this is some sort of clue?" he asked in bewilderment.

"I don't know," I said, suddenly feeling scared. "Is it possible Mr. Buxton could be involved in all of this?"

Lance shivered. "Mr. Buxton? Nah, he couldn't be! Could he, Willi?"

I stared again at the piece of blotter. There was Mr. Buxton's name, clear as day.

"I don't know, Lance," I said. "Maybe he could."

"Holy suffering hayfever!" cried Lance. "What have we gotten ourselves into?"

I phoned Andrea the second I got home and told her about our baffling discovery. She was as weirded out by it as we were, but she wisely cautioned that it was much too soon for any of us to jump to conclusions about what the clue meant. "I mean, what motive would Mr. Buxton have for framing Mr. Karch?" she asked. That calmed me down a little and enabled me to turn my attention to the next crisis of the day: dinner at Jennifer's.

At six-thirty sharp, I showed up at Jennifer's house in one of my nicest dresses. Jennifer appeared at the door in a simple black jumpsuit and let me in. She looked kind of tense and distracted.

"You better prepare yourself," she said as she ushered me into the vestibule, "because you're not going to believe what you see. It's like totally unreal."

In an instant, I knew exactly what she meant.

"Jennifer," I gasped, "where did all the junk go—all of Duke's butter molds and candle snuffers? This place looks like something out of *Happy Home* magazine."

And indeed it did. The hallways and floors were empty—and squeaky clean. The furniture was free of boxes. All the woodwork had been waxed and polished.

"Duke and I worked on the place all last night and for a couple of hours after I got home. Doesn't it look disgusting?"

"Well, it certainly looks, er, awfully *normal*," I said.

At that moment, Mr. Barnes entered the room.

"Hi, Willi," he said, his face lighting up. "I'm so happy you came. I haven't seen you in such a long while."

He came over and gave me a kiss on the cheek. I blushed. Mr. Barnes is so handsome. If he hadn't been some kind of computer genius, I swear he could have been a famous movie star—that's how gorgeous he is.

"Leona and Tessa will be here any minute," he said.

At precisely seven o'clock the doorbell rang, and we all hurried over to greet the Ramseys. Mrs. Ramsey, a slim, attractive woman, entered first. She was dressed to impress in a drop-dead dinner dress (that I thought was cut way too low) and a pair of dazzling pendant earrings that drew attention to the striking bones of her face. Tessa trudged in behind her like a condemned prisoner, scowling darkly. She had on a heather-blue skirt, matching sweater, and a string of tiny pearls, and was clutching a large, irregularly shaped gift wrapped in beautiful paper.

After a few moments of friendly chit-chat in the vestibule, Leona gave Tessa a gentle nudge.

"The present, dear," she said. "Give Jennifer her present."

Tessa glared at Jennifer and handed her the gift. "Here," she said sourly. "This is for you."

Grudgingly, Jennifer accepted it and returned a tepid smile. "Thanks," she said.

"Go on and open it," Leona said eagerly.

Jennifer set the heavy package down on the vestibule table and unwrapped it. It was a gorgeous amaryllis plant in a pretty porcelain pot.

I could tell Jennifer was touched, in spite of herself. She loved flowers and plants of all kinds. "It's really lovely, Mrs. Ramsey," she said. "Thank you."

Mr. Barnes smiled. "That was sweet of you, Leona—and you, too, Tessa. Now why don't we go in?"

Minutes later, the five of us were all sitting around the large oval table in the dining room. Tessa was on my right, Jennifer on my left. Across from us were Mr. Barnes and Mrs. Ramsey, talking and laughing together like old friends.

Soon, the kitchen door opened and Duke emerged, carrying a tureen of steaming soup. "Chicken noodle à la Duke!" he called out. He ladled out generous portions to everyone, then plunked himself down on a chair.

"Let's eat!" Mr. Barnes said. "I'm starved."

"Me, too," I said, trying to strike a cheery note.

Neither Tessa nor Jennifer said anything. They just looked past me, regarding each other stonily.

"Jennifer," Mrs. Ramsey began pleasantly, "Tessa tells me that you were a model before you came to Wellbie. Tessa would *love* to be a model someday. How did you like doing it?"

I could hear Tessa's teeth grinding at her mother's inadvertent revelation of one of her secret desires.

"It was okay," said Jennifer. She stared down into her bowl and said no more.

In fact, Mrs. Ramsey had asked the wrong question. For some dark reason, Jennifer hates talking about her modeling career—even to me. To this day, I still don't know whether her silence has something to do with her parents' divorce or with something that occurred during her career. Whatever it is, she always clams up whenever the subject comes up.

"What Jennifer means," Mr. Barnes hastened to add, " is that modeling had its good and bad points. She was incredibly successful—she was *Dazzle* magazine's 'Cover Girl of the Year' last year—but it was also a lot of work. Right, pumpkin?"

"Right," said Jennifer without elaborating.

"Mmm. This is great soup, Duke," I said loudly, hoping to change the subject.

"Glad you like it, Willi," Duke said proudly. "It's the peppered tree-ear fungus that gives it that special zing."

Tessa gagged, put her spoon down, and pushed her bowl away. "I'm finished, thank you," she said.

The meal that followed must have established some kind of a new world's record for quietness among fourteen-year-olds. Although Tessa and Jennifer maintained attitudes of formal politeness toward one another, Tessa barely spoke to Jennifer, and Jennifer barely acknowledged Tessa. Because I was stuck in the middle of them, I was the one who ended up having to relay back and forth all the biting remarks that they couldn't openly say to each other. Boy, was it exhausting!

"Willi, would you please tell Tessa to get her filthy sleeve out of the beet dish?" Jennifer whispered to me after the main course had been served.

"Willi, would you please tell Jennifer that she'll bloat up like a pig if she hogs all the salt?" Tessa said to me under her breath.

To which Jennifer replied, "Willi, would you please tell Tessa not to stare at me like that? Her zits are making me lose my appetite."

About fifteen times before dessert, Tessa mentioned her father, who still lives in Wellbie and is the highly successful president of the First Wellbie National Bank. About the same number of times, Jennifer brought up the issue of Mr. Barnes's upcoming business trip—about ten days off—and of how much she wanted to "spend some quality time" with Mr. Barnes *alone* before he left town.

Through it all, Tom and Leona seemed totally oblivious to what the two girls were doing. They spent most of the dinner laughing and joking about the various mishaps they'd had on their recent ice-skating date or talking about the work they were going to do on the PTA's Karch committee. They didn't provide me with any more leads, though. It sounded like the PTA knew less than I did.

By the time dessert was served, Tessa and Jennifer were pretty exhausted from their well-camouflaged sniping at each other and from trying to get through to their thick-skulled parents. Like two weary fighters who had battled to a tie, they even shook hands graciously at the door when it was time for the Ramseys to leave.

"It's been a *wonderful* evening, Tom," Leona said to Mr. Barnes as we all stood together in the frosty cold air on the porch. "Duke's dinner was divine. Your house is simply lovely, and so is your charming family. I hope we can do this again."

"That would be wonderful, Leona," Mr. Barnes said. "I'm sure Jennifer would like that too."

Jennifer was standing behind me. I heard her gasp in shock. Tessa was right in front of me. I saw her shudder.

Mrs. Ramsey and Tessa descended the porch steps and walked to their car.

After Tessa and Mrs. Ramsey had driven off, and Mr. Barnes and Duke had gone back into the house, Jennifer and I put on our jackets and took a long walk around the block to clear our brains.

"Whew!" I said. "I'm glad that's over. Aren't you?"

Jennifer nodded. "I hate her!"

"Who? Tessa?"

"No, Leona."

"I've got to be honest with you, Jennifer," I said as carefully as I could. "Leona didn't seem so bad to me."

"I know," Jennifer replied. "That's why I hate her. I'd been praying for days that Leona would turn out to be a witch—someone I could hate without feeling ashamed of myself. But she isn't a monster at all." Jennifer kicked a stone twenty feet down the street. "I hate it that she's nice. It doesn't give me an excuse to hate her the way I want to hate her. Do you know what I mean?"

"Perfectly. She didn't let you off the hook."

Jennifer nodded. "Yeah, that's it. I guess it's the same problem with Mr. Karch. Everybody wants him to be guilty because that would make everything neater and easier."

"Yeah," I said.

"What am I going to do, Willi?" Jennifer said in despair. "I just know that Dad and Mrs. Ramsey aren't meant for each other. Given enough time, I'm sure Dad would figure that out."

I stopped short. Jennifer had just given me an idea. "You know," I said, "There's only a short time left before your dad's got to leave. Suppose we could keep your dad and Mrs. Ramsey preoccupied during that period—so that they couldn't see each other so much. Do you think that might help?"

Jennifer thrust her hands into her jacket pockets. "It might," she said. "It would certainly cool things off in their relationship."

"I think I know a way we can arrange it," I said.

"How?" Jennifer asked. "What are you thinking of?"

"The Peace of Wellbie," I said.

"The Peace of WHAT?" Jennifer exclaimed. "I'm freaking out and you're thinking about history!"

"No, you don't understand," I said. "I'm talking about a temporary alliance between you and Tessa to keep your dad and her mom too busy to date until your dad leaves town."

Jennifer shook her head violently. "It'll never work."

"Why?"

"Tessa will never go for it."

I brushed back a lock of hair that had blown down over my eyes. "I think she might," I said. "For once, you both have a common purpose. After March seventeenth, the truce could end, and we could all go back to happily hating each other."

"It's totally crazy," Jennifer said. "Tessa will never cooperate."

I persisted. "I know Andrea would help. She told me last week she wanted to do something to keep you and Tessa from tearing each other apart."

Jennifer raised her eyebrows. "She did?"

"Uh-huh," I said.

We walked in silence for a while, then Jennifer said, "So let me get this straight. You're proposing a peace treaty that would involve Tessa and me?"

"Right, and it would be policed by me and Andrea."

"It still won't solve the problem of the PTA committee. Dad and Mrs. Ramsey could still meet there."

"No," I said. "But if Lance and I can prove that Mr. Karch is innocent, the committee won't need to exist anymore. And if there's no committee, there's no reason for your dad and Leona to meet there."

"Did you turn up any clues today in the auditorium?" Jennifer asked.

I took a deep breath. "We turned up something," I said, "but I'm not sure what it means. Our phantom letter-writer left us an envelope with the name of someone from our school on a scrap of paper."

"How odd," Jennifer said. "Whose name was it?"

I shivered slightly as I remembered the words that were written on the piece of blotter.

"Mr. Buxton's," I replied grimly.

Chapter 9

On Friday morning, I grabbed Andrea while *The Real McCoy* was being distributed during homeroom, and told her about my idea of arranging a ten-day cease-fire between Tessa and Jennifer. She loved it immediately and suggested that the four of of us meet somewhere on neutral territory after school to work out the exact details. We decided to go to the Caboose Diner, because it has large, private booths and it served the best ice-cream sodas and sundaes in town. It also happened to be owned by the Twerp's family. I started wondering if there was any way to get free ice cream from the Twerp.

Jennifer and I were already halfway through our ice-cream floats when Tessa and Andrea arrived. Tessa gave us a tight-lipped smile and slid onto the high-backed bench across from us. Andrea sat down next to her and placed her briefcase on the table.

"Where's Lance?" Andrea asked, gazing around.

I pointed to the counter at the other end of the diner, where the Twerp was in the process of serving a cup of coffee and a Danish to Turk Guffey.

"He's working?" Andrea said.

"His dad nailed him when we walked in," I said. "Mr. Kirkwood's short on help today. So he's making Lance fill in."

"It's just as well," Andrea said, popping open the locks on her briefcase. "We've got some serious business to transact."

I nodded in agreement.

Lifting the lid slightly, Andrea withdrew a silver ballpoint pen and a yellow legal pad with lots of notes scribbled all over it.

"For the sake of smooth negotiations," she said, "I suggest, Willi, that you do all the talking for your client and I do all the talking for mine. Are we agreed?"

"What do you think, Jennifer?" I asked.

Jennifer lifted the maraschino cherry out of her glass and twirled it by the stem. "I'm perfectly willing to let you and Willi lead this discussion," she said to Andrea, "but I always reserve the right to speak for myself."

"Me too," demanded Tessa.

"Good. Now, let's see," Andrea said, adjusting her glasses and squinting at the pad. "I have some general principles here, and some draft language I'd like to read. Tell me what you think of it."

Andrea started reading from the yellow pad:

WE, THE UNDERSIGNED, JENNIFER CAUSE-
WELL BARNES AND TESSA APHRODITE RAMSEY—

"Aphrodite?" Jennifer said, putting her hand over her mouth and giggling. "I never knew your middle name was *Aphrodite*."

"Shut up, *Barnsey*!" Tessa snarled.

"You want to make something of it?" Jennifer retorted.

Andrea pounded the table. "Willi, will you *please* control your client?"

I turned to Jennifer. "Andrea's right," I said. "That remark was uncalled for, Jennifer. Just cool it."

Jennifer slumped back in her seat. "Okay, okay— I'm sorry."

"Thank you, counselor," Andrea said to me. "Now, as I was saying when I was interrupted: 'We, the undersigned, blah, blah, blah—'

> . . . HEREBY AGREE TO SET ASIDE OUR DIFFERENCES AND BE NICE TO EACH OTHER FOR ONE WEEK. DURING SUCH TIME, WE SHALL TAKE ALL NECESSARY ACTIONS TO ENSURE THAT THE FRIENDSHIP BETWEEN OUR PARENTS DOESN'T GET ANY FRIENDLIER, SO THAT WE, THE UNDERSIGNED, CAN CONTINUE TO REMAIN BEST OF ENEMIES FOREVER MORE.

"Well, do you like it?" Andrea asked, passing me the pad.

I studied the agreement. "Geez, Andrea," I said. "This sounds so official—like you had your lawyer draw it up."

"Thanks," said Andrea, beaming proudly.

Jennifer leaned over and whispered something into my ear.

"My client has a question," I said. "If she signs this, does she literally have to be *nice* to your client for a week or merely *not un-nice*?"

After conferring with Tessa, Andrea cleared her throat and said, "My client agrees. She says it's asking too much of her to be nice to Jennifer for a week. With your permission we'll cross out the word *nice* and replace it with *not un-nice*."

Jennifer nodded yes, and I made the changes in the wording.

"Any other problems?" Andrea asked.

Jennifer raised her hand. "My dad's leaving for Los Angeles on March seventeenth—eight days from today. The contract should say that the truce expires then, not just in a week."

"Any objection, Tessa?" I asked.

"None," she replied.

"Good," I said and made that correction too. We were making great progress.

The Twerp slipped away from the counter for a couple of minutes to see how things were going and to take Andrea's and Tessa's orders.

"You really ought to try the peacemakers' special today," he said with a totally straight face. "It's two scoops of Rocky Road smothered in Good Humor."

I crumpled a napkin and threw it at him. "Boo! Hiss!" I cried. "Go away!"

Lance ducked my shot and laughed. He jotted down Tessa's and Andrea's orders, then scooted off.

"May I speak now?" Tessa asked impatiently.

"Floor's yours," said Jennifer.

"Finally," Tessa grumped. "Listen," she said. "I want to know what we're actually going to be doing over the next eight days." Her eyes shifted from Andrea to Jennifer to me. "Now, I know I can make a wreck of Mom's social calendar if I put my mind to it. That's no sweat. And I suppose Jennifer can do the same with her dad's. But what are we going to do about the Karch committee? That's where I get off. I don't want to have anything to do with saving Gaylord Karch's neck."

I glanced at Andrea with alarm. I didn't know that Tessa knew that we were trying to prove Mr. Karch's innocence.

"It's all right, Willi," Andrea said. "I told Tessa about the R.M.S.I.U."

"I've got a confession to make, too," I said, somewhat sheepishly. "I told Jennifer about what we were doing, too."

Andrea laughed. "I guess that means there are no secrets from anyone."

Just then, the Twerp appeared with a small dish of low-cal Cowardly Crunch for Andrea and a big Marshmallow Mountain Mudslide for Tessa. Andrea asked Lance to stick around for a few minutes, and we quickly discussed the Karch issue and decided that it shouldn't be included in the peace treaty. We all agreed that Jennifer and Tessa shouldn't try to obstruct the work of their parents on the PTA committee. Lance and I promised that we would step up our investigatory efforts and that we would pay a call on Mr. Karch tomorrow.

That pleased everyone. Then the historic moment came.

"Willi," Andrea asked solemnly, "is your client ready to sign the treaty?"

I looked at Jennifer, and she nodded her head.

"We are, counselor," I said.

Then it was my turn to ask the question. "Andrea, is your client ready to sign the agreement?"

Andrea glanced at Tessa, who shrugged and said, "Let's get this thing over with."

"We're ready, counselor," Andrea replied.

"Shall we have a simultaneous signing?" I asked, handing pens to Jennifer and Tessa.

Jennifer and Tessa stood up and leaned over the document, pens poised.

"Ready," I said. "One, two, three—sign!"

Two pens made furious scratching noises on the yellow pad, and the deed was done! Andrea and I witnessed the document, then leaped up to congratulate our friends.

"Operation Disrupt is offically launched," Andrea said.

"Hold on!" Lance cried. "Something's missing."

"What?" I asked.

"Aren't you going to seal it in blood or something? That's how they do it in the movies."

"Ugh, you're so gross, Lance!" I said.

"Okay then, forget it," he said. "No blood." He paused and gave me one of his deadpan looks. "How about a drop of ketchup instead?"

At that, we all grabbed handfuls of napkins and began pelting the Twerp mercilessly until he beat a hasty retreat.

When we left the diner shortly after, we were all proud of our achievement. The Truce of the Caboose had been signed! The impossible had occurred: Jennifer Causewell Barnes and Tessa Aphrodite Ramsey had temporarily buried the hatchet and become the best of enemies.

Chapter 10

Mr. Karch lives alone in a cottage at the end of Pudding Lane on the west side of Wellbie, not far from the Piggly-Wiggly where Tessa's mom and Jennifer's dad had their fateful encounter in the dairy section. On Saturday morning, Mom drove me over to the Piggly-Wiggly to meet Lance, who had insisted that we rendezvous there and walk over to Gaylord's house together. Lance said it was important for us to go over as a team so that we could present "a united front." Frankly, I thought it was because he was too scared of what might happen if he showed up at the cottage first and had to deal with Gaylord by himself. I didn't say anything to him, though. Boys—even twerps—have their pride.

Shortly after Mom dropped me off, Lance came hustling up the street. I was glad he wasn't late because the weather was freezing, and I could feel the cold biting through my ratty old down jacket.

"Hi, Willi," he said. "You ready?"

"As I'll ever be," I said.

The Twerp took a deep breath. "Okay," he said, "let's go."

Hunching our shoulders against the bitter wind, we crossed Main Street, walked four blocks west on Elm, and turned right onto Pudding Lane.

"I heard a report on the radio this morning about the school board's investigation," Lance said.

"What did it say?"

"Nothing good. According to the report, they haven't been able to turn up any evidence backing up Mr. Karch's claims."

"Well, maybe they're not working on the same leads as we are," I said. "Don't let it get you down."

"It's hard not to," he said glumly. "When I was working behind the counter at the diner yesterday, a bunch of people were talking about Mr. Karch. Turk Guffey said that he didn't feel sorry for Mr. Karch one bit. He said Mr. Karch acted 'high and mighty' to him all the time and that he always bullied Emma in class. I waited for someone to defend Gaylord, but no one did."

"You can't let something like that affect your judgment," I said. "We're investigative reporters. We deal in facts, not opinion."

As we approached the white picket fence that surrounded Gaylord's front yard, Lance turned to me and said, "You know, Willi, right now I wish I hadn't written that story."

"I know," I said. "I wish I'd been a little less eager to want to teach Mr. Karch a lesson. But we can't take back what's happened. We should look on the bright side."

"What bright side?"

"Well, maybe there was something in your article that caused 'A CONCERNED STUDENT' to write us those notes. Maybe those notes will help us to clear Mr. Karch's name. It's still possible that something good will come out of your article."

"You really think so?"

"If I didn't, I wouldn't be doing an insane thing like coming to Mr. Karch's house today." I opened the gate to Mr. Karch's front yard, and we walked up the flagstone path to the door.

"You ring and I'll stand off to one side," said Lance. "If he sees you first, there'll be less bloodshed."

"Stop it, Lance," I said. "You're gonna make me more nervous than I already am. Nothing's going to happen."

I pushed the doorbell and prayed.

As the chimes sounded, Lance flipped up the collar on his coat and buried his chin in his chest in a feeble attempt at disguise.

Moments later, Mr. Karch appeared at the door, wearing a brown corduroy jacket with leather patches at the elbows. He scrutinized both of us, Lance especially. It was clear he was surprised to see us.

"Yes, Wilhelmina?" he said. "Have you and the joking journalist stopped by to apologize? Or merely to gather dirt for your newspaper's next humor piece?"

I lowered my eyes and blushed. "You've got every reason to be mad at us, Mr. Karch," I said.

"We're both really sorry about the article. We didn't mean it to be hurtful or anything."

"Th-that's right, sir," the Twerp stammered. "I-I'm real sorry about what I wrote."

Mr. Karch narrowed his eyes. I couldn't tell if he was going to accept our apologies or slam the door in our faces.

"I want you both to know one thing," he said sternly. "I don't mind if you make fun of me. But I deeply resent it when you make fun of math. Math is the poetry of the mind—the highest form of thought. If more students learned math the way *I* teach it, there would be fewer mush-minds in the world."

"I know, sir," I said. "We apologize if we insulted math."

Mr. Karch stared at us for a little while longer. "All right," he said, "I accept your apologies. Now, is that all? I've got a lot of things to do." He started to close the door.

"Wait!" I said. "There is something else."

Mr. Karch's eyebrows lifted. "Yes, what is it?"

"Lance and I are working on an article about your case. We believe that someone in school may have evidence that can prove your innocence. We're doing investigative work to try and come up with that evidence. So we were wondering if we could come in and ask you a few questions."

Mr. Karch looked at me warily. "This isn't just a clever ruse to do another *Real McCoy* hatchet job, is it?"

"I promise it isn't," I said.

"This is *really* on the level, sir," added Lance.

Mr. Karch thought for a while, then said, "All right, you may come in. But I don't see what can be gained by it. I've gone over all of these matters with the school board before and nothing seems to have come of it. No one's turned up anything."

Mr. Karch escorted us into his living room. It was a sad-looking, sparely furnished room with no rugs on the floor and no paintings or decorations on the walls. It had one couch, one coffee table, one floor lamp, one reading chair and one huge bookcase (filled exclusively with books about math) that covered an entire wall.

Lance and I took seats on the couch. Mr. Karch sat down in his reading chair.

"Okay, what is it that you'd like to know?" Mr. Karch asked.

I took out a small spiral notebook.

"Mr. Karch," I began, "do you have any papers or documents lying around your house that could prove you went to Witherspoon College? It could be anything—pictures, old sweatshirts, your college yearbook."

"If I did, don't you think I would have given that information to the school board?"

"You mean you don't have *anything*?" Lance asked, incredulous.

"Young man, I am a *math* teacher. I believe in logic and precision, not childish sentimentality. The past means nothing to me. I threw out all my college mementos years ago."

Okay, scratch that possibility, I thought.

"What about friends?" I asked. "Do you still keep in touch with any friends from college who could testify on your behalf?"

"Friends?" Mr. Karch replied. "I went to college to get an education, not to make friends. I spent most of my time in the library."

I didn't show it, but I was shocked. I couldn't imagine how anyone could say that. My life would be so empty without Jennifer or any of my other friends.

"What about clubs or extracurricular activities?" Lance asked. "Were you on the school newspaper? Did you go out for any sports or anything?"

"I detest all sports," Mr. Karch said. "But now that you mention it, I did belong to one club. However, I don't see how that could matter much. I only belonged for a brief time."

"Which one was it?" Lance asked. "The math club?"

"No, the glee club. I've always had a lovely tenor voice."

I nearly burst out laughing. The thought of Mr. Karch in the *glee* club was just too funny for words. I managed to control myself, though. "Do you happen to remember the names of anybody in the glee club?" I asked.

"Only Orville Truitt," Mr. Karch said. "He stood in front of me. He had a scratchy, annoying voice. They never should have accepted him."

"Try to think, Mr. Karch," I said. "Do you have any idea where he lives? Maybe we could get in touch with him. It could be important."

Mr. Karch thought for a while. "It was someplace far away. Aha! Now I recall. Anchorage, Alaska."

"That's great!" I exclaimed, jotting the information down. "This is very helpful. We'll try to track him down."

I looked at Lance. "Do you have any more questions?"

The Twerp shook his head.

"Okay," I said. "Then let me ask you just one more. Mr. Karch, do you know of anyone—in school or otherwise—who would want to get you into trouble?" *Like Mr. Buxton*, I thought.

"No," Mr. Karch said. "I don't know anyone like that."

"That's it," I said, closing my notebook. "Thank you for talking with us."

Mr. Karch was much more cordial to us when he showed us out than he'd been when we'd arrived. But his mood remained pessimistic. "I appreciate your taking an interest in my case," he said. "But I doubt whether you'll find Orville; he'll probably have disappeared, just like all my records."

As Lance and I headed back to the Piggly-Wiggly to call Mom to pick us up, a plan of action began hatching in my mind. I turned to Lance and said, "I want you to call information in Anchorage. See if you can get Orville Truitt's phone number. Then call him up and ask him if he remembers Mr. Karch. If he does, find out if he's willing to testify that he went to college with Mr. Karch."

"Roger," said Lance.

103

I was excited. We'd come up with a promising lead that nobody else had uncovered!

Andrea Wellbie put it best when I spoke to her on the phone as soon as I got home. "With Orville Truitt's help," she said, "we can crack this case wide open."

Chapter 11

Sunday afternoon is usually practice time for Dave's band, Slippery Slop. That's why it's usually the time Dad, Mom, and I make plans to be out of the house. Take it from me, you don't want to be in the same time zone as Dave when he starts playing "Mouse for Lunch," or any of his other garbage punk compositions. His music has all the charm of a fingernail being scraped across a blackboard. It actually gives me hives. I'll never understand why Slippery Slop has suddenly become so popular in town.

When I stumbled down to breakfast on Sunday morning, Dad was announcing his evacuation plans. He was going over to the Wellbie public library to do some research on an article he was writing for *Modern Dentist Magazine* on the history of American mouthwash.

I'd already decided what I wanted to do. I'd seen in the newspaper that Murphy's department store was having a sale on down coats and jackets. Remembering how cold I'd been yesterday waiting for Lance outside the Piggly-Wiggly, I asked Mom if she would take me down to the mall so that I could buy a new jacket.

"What's wrong with the one you've got?" Mom asked.

I went to the hall closet, took my jacket out and showed Mom the tattered lining and a tear along one seam.

"Nobody would take this even if I gave it away," I said, poking my fingers through the hole.

"Okay," Mom said. "You win. We'll go to Murphy's after lunch. Do you think Jennifer might want to come along? The two of you could pick out a jacket while I look at rugs."

That was a great idea. Even though Jennifer downplays her former modeling career and is the least clothes-crazed girl I know (maybe it's because everything looks great on her), she's never lost her model's eye for clothes. If she went along, Mom wouldn't force me to get one of those "practical" jackets that make me look like the Goodyear blimp.

I dashed upstairs and called Jennifer immediately. When she got on the line, I was surprised to hear how cheery she sounded.

"Jennifer," I said. "What's up? You sound happier than I've heard you in weeks."

"I am," she said excitedly. "Our plan is working."

"The peace treaty?"

"Uh-huh. Operation Disrupt has begun. On Friday night, Leona canceled a dinner date with Dad. Tessa had come down with a 'bad stomachache.' "

"Oh," I chuckled, "the old stomachache routine. It works like a charm."

"Then yesterday," Jennifer continued, "I threw a homework freakout. I showed Dad the biology quiz I flunked on Wednesday. I told him I was falling behind in class and that I needed emergency help to pass my midterms. Dad got real worried and sat me down with my books at the kitchen table. We went over cell division and photosynthesis for the entire evening. When Leona called to ask if he wanted to go to the movies, he told her he couldn't because he had to help me."

"What about today?"

"That's covered too. Duke and Dad are visiting friends in Iowa City. They won't be back until late." Jennifer paused abruptly. "Gee, Willi," she said. "I've been hogging the whole conversation. You haven't said a word about yesterday. I'm dying to hear about your interview with Mr. Karch."

"Well . . ." I said, and proceeded to tell her the latest news flash from Pudding Lane. Jennifer laughed when I got to the part about Mr. Karch and the glee club, but she quickly grasped the importance of the Oliver Truitt lead. "If you and the Twerp can locate this guy," she said, "you could be the first ones to show Mr. Karch didn't lie about attending college."

"That's a big 'if'," I said.

"Has Lance found anything out yet?"

"I don't know," I said. "He hasn't called me."

"Gee, I hope you don't wind up sitting by the phone all day."

"You must be kidding," I said. "Dave's band is coming over for rehearsal today. I'm getting out of here. In fact, that's the reason I'm calling. I need to buy a jacket at Murphy's. You want to come?"

"Sure," she said with a laugh. "It's a *wonderful* day for shopping—for doing practically anything."

For those who love—and live—to shop, the indoor Wellbie Mall is shopping heaven. It's got twenty stores, five fast-food restaurants, a six-plex cinema, an aerobics salon, a great video rental place, three fountains, and two flower gardens—all under one roof. Murphy's is the largest store in the mall, and the place where you can find the best bargains.

Shortly after we arrived at Murphy's, Mom announced that she was going up to the rug department on the third floor. She would meet us at the Outdoor Shop, where the down jackets were on sale, in precisely an hour and a half. Jennifer and I had loads of time, so we wandered around the store for a while, looking at earrings and lingerie and then at spring blouses and skirts.

"I have an idea," Jennifer said mischievously when we were in the middle of the women's department. "Let's see who can come up with the most horribly mismatched outfit." She grabbed a couple of ugly blouses and skirts off a rack and made a beeline for the dressing room.

"Hey, wait up," I said, grabbing the dorkiest things I could find and tearing after her.

When we emerged from the dressing booths five minutes later, it was clear that Jennifer had won the contest, hands-down. She had on a frilly yellow floral-print blouse and a mid-length navy-blue skirt adorned with large orange polka dots. The clash was horrendous. My hasty selection—a red pin-striped blouse with a magenta pleated skirt—didn't even come close.

As we stood in front of the mirrors, admiring our weird combinations, I realized how happy I was that Jennifer was slowly coming back to her old self again. I had missed that spark of wacky playfulness that made our friendship so wonderfully unpredictable.

We returned the clothes to their racks and walked over to the Outdoor Shop, which was swarming with bargain hunters. The down jackets were at the far end of the shop along a long display window that looked out onto the main promenade of the mall.

"What do you think?" I said, slipping on a canary yellow jacket and modeling it for Jennifer's inspection.

Jennifer eyed it carefully and shook her head. "Much too bulky in the shoulders," she said. "It makes you look like a football player."

After I chose two others, which also failed to meet her approval, she frowned and said, "I'll tell you what, Willi. You keep looking here. I'll go check out the ski jackets. They're more stylish. What size are you, anyway, a five junior?"

I nodded and Jennifer strode off to the ski jacket section, which was two aisles down, near the entrance to the promenade.

I continued searching the racks and finally found

a jacket I liked, with jazzy colors, great pockets, and a detachable hood. I took it over to the ski section to show Jennifer, but she wasn't there.

I stared out the display window, wondering where Jennifer had gone. Suddenly I saw her sitting on a bench in the middle of the promenade. Then I noticed another girl sitting beside her. It was Emma Guffey, and she looked pretty upset about something. I dropped my jacket at the sales desk for safekeeping and ran out to join them.

Jennifer's face brightened as I approached. She seemed almost relieved to see me. "Oh, Willi," she said, "I'm glad you found me. Emma saw me in the shop and asked if I could talk with her for a few minutes out here. She says she's got some kind of a family problem and needs some advice."

I froze on the spot. I remembered all too well what had happened last year when Jennifer launched her campaign against "Dear Heart." To give "Dear Heart" competition she'd set up a table in the corner of the cafeteria ("Jennifer's Corner") and offered advice to anyone who wanted it. She soon discovered, though, that helping kids with their problems was much harder than she'd thought. When she shut down "Jennifer's Corner," she swore that she would never go back into the advice business again. Was she considering breaking her pledge?

It was Emma who gave me my answer. Turning to me with her sad, puppy-dog eyes, she said, "Willi, you're Jennifer's friend. Maybe you can persuade her. I've asked her to reopen 'Jennifer's

Corner' for me—just this once. But she won't. Maybe you can convince her to change her mind."

I glanced at Jennifer. She was shaking her head.

"What's the problem?" I asked Emma, breathing easier now that I knew that Jennifer was holding fast to her promise.

"It's a personal matter," Emma said. "It concerns my family." Her eyes grew shiny as she fought back tears. "I've never asked anyone for help before, but I need some advice fast."

"Why don't you speak with the guidance counselor," I suggested.

"I can't," Emma said, staring at the ground.

"Why not?"

"I just can't. I don't need *official* advice from a guidance counselor. I need *unofficial* advice from someone I can trust. That's why I asked Jennifer."

Jennifer slipped her arm around the girl's shoulder and said, "Look, Emma, I'd really like to help you, but your problem sounds serious. I learned my lesson about making snap judgments about kids' problems. If you really want my advice, I advise you to write a letter to 'Dear Heart.'"

I couldn't believe my ears. Did I actually hear Jennifer Barnes tell Emma to write a letter to "Dear Heart"? I guess Jennifer has come a long way since the days of "Jennifer's Corner."

Emma perked up immediately at Jennifer's suggestion. "You know," she said, "I'd never thought about 'Dear Heart.' Do you think 'Dear Heart' would answer me?"

"What's your guess, Willi?" Jennifer asked me. "You know more about this than me."

"Well, of course, you can never be sure with 'Dear Heart,'" I said carefully. "But I have a strong hunch that your letter will be answered."

Minutes later, Mom showed up, looking tired and cross. We hadn't met her in the Outdoor Shop at the agreed-upon time, and she'd been searching high and low for us. As Mom started lecturing me on the virtues of punctuality, Emma quietly waved goodbye and slipped away into the vast shopping caverns of the Wellbie Mall. I couldn't help wondering as she disappeared from view what her disturbing family problem might be, and how I, as "Dear Heart," might be able to help.

After Mom finished her speech, I waited for a reasonable amount of time for her to cool down. Then I calmly explained that Jennifer and I hadn't been goofing off all this time, that we'd only come out here to help Emma and that I'd already picked out a jacket I liked back at the Outdoor Shop.

The stern expression on Mom's face softened. With a sigh, she pulled out a Murphy's credit card and said, "Okay, girls. Charge!" With that, we all linked arms and marched back into Murphy's, and Mom bought me the jazzy-looking down jacket that had caught my eye earlier.

By the time we dropped Jennifer off and returned home ourselves, it was nearly five o'clock. The Slippery Slop jam session was over, and Dave was alone in the house. As I headed up stairs,

Dave said, "Some guy named Lance called. He said you should call him back right away. Does Robbie know you're two-timing him?"

"Shut up," I said, and ran upstairs. When I hit the landing, I grabbed the hall phone and took it into my room. Then I jumped onto my bed and anxiously dialed the Twerp's number.

"I've got some bad news and some good news," the Twerp reported to me moments later. "The bad news is that Oliver Truitt doesn't remember Mr. Karch at all, which means he can't testify that Mr. Karch went to college with him."

"Oh great," I said, disappointed. "What's the good news?"

"The good news is that he's still got his freshman yearbook. I asked him to check in it, and he said it's got a picture of Mr. Karch."

When I heard this, I let out a loud whoop. "Way to go, Lance!" I exclaimed. "Now we've really got something. Is he going to make a copy of the page and send it to us?" I asked eagerly.

"Better than that. He's sending us the yearbook by express mail. We should get it by Tuesday. Now, is that great or what?"

"It's fantastic, Lance," I said. "I'm really proud of you. Have you told Andrea yet?"

"Uh-huh. She wants us to have a meeting as soon as the package comes."

After I hung up the phone, I lay on my bed thinking for a long while. I thought about Jennifer and Mr. Karch and about the weird games fortune had been playing with their lives. A week ago,

Jennifer was an emotional wreck, freaked out by the fear that her worst enemy might become her stepsister. Now, Jennifer was joining forces with that same bitter enemy in an effort to make sure that never happened. Two weeks ago, Mr. Karch was at the peak of his career. He'd just been nominated for the state's highest math award. A week after that, his name was mud, and he seemed headed for certain dismissal. Now (thanks to Lance and me), his fortune seemed about to take a turn for the better again.

Who would have thought all these strange things could happen? Will wonders never cease?

Chapter 12

On Monday, I checked the "Dear Heart" box after school and found two letters inside, which I stuffed into my knapsack and took home with me. I knew as soon as I read them that neither of them was from Emma. One was written by a sophomore boy who wanted to take Mrs. Jasper's cooking class next fall but was afraid of what the other boys might think. The second was from a girl calling herself "Peaches" who wanted to fix her best friend up with her older brother, and wondered if that was a good idea. "Peaches" wasn't Emma because Emma doesn't have a brother. After reading the letters, I scribbled a few notes to myself in the margins, then slipped them into a folder on my desk for answering tomorrow.

I wondered whether Emma was going to finish her letter in time. Jennifer had mentioned it to me in gym today that Emma had said she was having trouble writing it. My copy deadline was Thursday morning. If Emma's letter wasn't in the box by Wednesday, there would be no chance that I could squeeze it into next week's "Dear Heart" column. I didn't know how serious her problem was, but if it really was urgent, I didn't want her to wait too long for an answer.

At lunch on Tuesday, Jennifer came in a little late and sat down next to me. "Ugh," she said, staring at her bowl of oily minestrone soup. "This is the worst excuse for minestrone I've ever seen. They could make motor oil out of it."

"Don't bother with the ravioli, either," I said. "It's way overcooked."

"You know, Willi," Jennifer said, waving her spoon in my face for emphasis, "somebody ought to do something about the food in this school. It's becoming positively life-threatening."

"What do you have in mind?" I asked.

"Pickets, boycotts, a mass walkout."

"I don't know if I'd go that far," I said, laughing. "But I do know that Andrea's planning on doing a story in the newspaper about it—with a poll and everything."

"Well, it's about time," Jennifer said, and tore open a package of crackers, which I supposed was going to be her entire meal.

"Oh, speaking of the newspaper," Jennifer said, "Emma told me she finished her letter to 'Dear Heart.' "

"That's good," I said.

"She said she put it into the 'Dear Heart' box this morning. She looks relieved it's over with."

"I'll bet," I said.

116

"Now it's old 'Dear Heart's' headache, not ours," Jennifer said, grinning broadly.

"Yeah," I said, poking my ravioli with a fork and noticing that water gushed out the holes. "By the way," I said, changing the subject, "what's the latest news on Operation Disrupt?"

"You know," said Jennifer, "I think something interesting is happening between Dad and Mrs. Ramsey."

"Like what?"

"I'm not totally sure. But last night, Dad and Leona had their PTA Karch committee meeting and when Dad came back, I heard him grumbling to Duke about Leona."

"Really?" I asked, my ears pricking up. "About what?"

"Well, I think they had some kind of argument about Mr. Karch. It seems Leona said that Mr. Karch should be dismissed and Dad said that he shouldn't."

I reached for my milk carton and tugged on the spout. "Does anybody actually *do* anything on that committee?" I asked.

"As far as I can tell, only Dad and Leona really know anything about the issues. The rest of the committee members just sit around drinking coffee and eating donuts."

"Oh brother!" I said. "They might as well not have a committee."

"That's what I think."

Just then, the spout on my carton gave way, spilling milk onto my tray. "How is all this going to affect Operation Disrupt?"

"Here," Jennifer said, handing me a wad of napkins. She gave a toss of her long black hair and continued, "It's not going to change things at all. Tessa and I are going to go ahead with our plans. There are only four more days left, counting today. I always had a gut feeling that Dad and Leona weren't meant for each other. Maybe they're finding that out now. But we can't get too overconfident."

"Is tonight your night or Tessa's night?"

"Mine," said Jennifer, polishing off her last cracker. "Jim mentioned to me this morning that his computer keyboard was broken, so I called Dad before I came to lunch—that's why I was late—and asked him if he would take a look at it this evening. Dad loves to talk about computers, and so does Jim. So Jim will bring the keyboard over, and that'll take up the whole evening."

"That was a smart move."

The five-minute warning bell rang in the cafeteria, signaling the end of the lunch period. Kids began dumping their trash into the garbage and shuffling out into the halls.

"You think you could come over too?" she asked, pushing her chair back and getting up.

"No," I said, "not if they're going to be talking computers. Besides, I've got too many things to do for the paper this week. I don't know when I'm going to find the time to do them all."

"Okay, I was just asking," said Jennifer. "I forgot that you've got the Karch thing."

I nodded. And I would also have another "Dear

118

Heart" letter to answer, I thought to myself, just as soon as I stopped by and looked in the box.

After dinner that night, I went up to my room, hung a "Do Not Disturb" sign on my doorknob and locked the door behind me. It was time to write "Dear Heart." I was already set up for my weekly writing ritual. On the night table next to my bed I'd carefully laid out everything a writer needs: sharp pencils, a brand-new writing pad, a big bowl of nacho-flavored potato chips, a family-size package of Vanilla Supreme Cookies and a bottle of Uncle Zeke's diet cream soda. On my bed, I'd arranged three of the four letters I wanted to answer in a neat pile. The fourth, which I hadn't read yet, was still in my knapsack. It was the letter I'd found in the "Dear Heart" box today—the letter I knew was Emma's.

I drank a tall glass of Uncle Zeke's and sat down crossed-legged on the bed with my pad in my lap. I took the first letter off the pile and popped a mind-sharpening Vanilla Supreme Cookie into my mouth. At last I was ready to begin.

Six Vanilla Supremes, a half-bowl of potato chips, and three glasses of cream soda later, I'd finished writing replies to all the letters in the pile. Now it was time to read and answer the last one—Emma's. Rather than trying to find it the slow way, I grabbed my knapsack and dumped its contents onto the bed. As I rummaged through the heap of tissues, hairbrushes, lipsticks, breath fresheners, crumpled homework papers, and loose change, I spotted the corners of two envelopes sticking out of the debris. I pulled them both out and set them down on my pad.

I recognized the first envelope immediately. It was the one from "A CONCERNED STUDENT" that I'd thrown into my knapsack when Mr. Buxton had unexpectedly interrupted our meeting at *The Real McCoy* office last week. The second letter was addressed "TO DEAR HEART."

As I glanced idly at the two envelopes, my eyes suddenly bugged out. *Could it be?* I thought. No, it was impossible. I took an emergency bite of a Vanilla Supreme Cookie to calm myself down. I thought I must be going crazy, or that my eyes were playing tricks on me.

The handwriting on both envelopes was IDENTICAL!

With my heart pounding, I opened Emma's letter and quickly double-checked it against the one "A CONCERNED STUDENT" had written to Andrea. There was no doubt about it. They'd been written by the same person. That could only mean one thing: Emma Guffey was none other than "A CONCERNED STUDENT," our phantom letter writer! *She* was the one who had the information that could clear Gaylord Karch's name!

I studied her letter closely. It read:

Dear Heart:
    Somebody in my family played a bad trick on another person recently. He felt that that person was picking on me in

school. I know he did it because he loves me and wants to protect me, but what he did was still wrong. I feel awful about it. I know how I can make things better for the person who got hurt, but I don't want the member of my family to get hurt either. I'm so confused. Tell me what I should do.

Broken up

P.S.: Please don't print this letter, just give me your answer!!

All at once, everything made sense. Our culprit was Emma's father, Turk Guffey. I remembered all the times that Jennifer, Lance, or I had heard Turk Guffey bad-mouthing Mr. Karch. He had a motive—his belief that Mr. Karch was picking on Emma—and he had the means. As the school maintenance man, Turk has unrestricted access to every room in the school. He could have easily sneaked into the main office after hours and taken Mr. Karch's college records from his files. I had a hunch that Emma knew exactly where those records were hidden and that, as "A CONCERNED STUDENT," she'd been trying to give us clues where to find them.

I chugged down another glass of cream soda and stared blankly at the walls of my room. I was in a real predicament. I'd just solved the mystery of who framed Gaylord Karch, but I didn't have any hard proof. To make matters worse, one of the key pieces of evidence I did have—Emma's letter—had been given to "Dear Heart" in strict confidence, and I couldn't betray that trust. I wanted to help Mr. Karch (and get my journalistic scoop), but I didn't necessarily want to get Turk into hot water if I could avoid it. I knew that Emma would be totally crushed if that happened—especially if she felt she was to blame for it.

After mulling the problem over for a while, I had an idea. Maybe "Dear Heart" *could* help. I wrote Emma the following reply:

> Confidential to "Broken Up":
> I think you know what's the right thing to do. If you can right the wrong that was done, you ought to do it as quickly as possible. Then you should sit down and talk to your family member and tell him, as gently as possible, that it was wrong for him to do a bad thing—even out of love for you.
>
> D.H.

I was hoping against hope that Emma would read my reply and put the documents back in their rightful place. That would certainly stop all the school board actions against Mr. Karch and restore him to the classroom. Not only that, it just might save Turk Guffey's neck.

* * *

Ten minutes later, as I was brushing all the potato chip and cookie crumbs off my bedspread, Andrea called me up in a state of excitement. She said that Lance had received Oliver Truitt's yearbook in the mail and he was going to bring it to school tomorrow.

"I'm scheduling a meeting of the R.M.S.I.U. for three-fifteen PM tomorrow," Andrea said. "It's crucial that you make it."

For an instant, I debated telling her about Emma's letter and my shocking discovery, but decided against it. I'd never revealed the name of a "Dear Heart" source to anyone, not even to Andrea. She, above all people, understood and appreciated my discretion.

"I'll be there," I said simply.

"Good," she replied. "I'm counting on you. And Willi—?"

"Yes?"

"You've done great work. After you write your story, I'm sure there'll be a promotion waiting for you."

I thanked Andrea and hung up. At this point, I wasn't even sure there was going to *be* a story. If all went well, Gaylord's records would soon mysteriously reappear, and nobody would be the wiser. People would probably blame it on some bureaucratic error or office mixup and let it go at that. I couldn't write a hard-hitting investigative story about that! And I surely couldn't tell anyone what I *really* knew because I'd only wind up getting Turk into trouble.

Just like Emma, I was trying to do the right thing. Only, in my case, doing the right thing probably meant saying goodbye to my long-sought promotion.

Chapter 13

Standing at the head of the work table in *The Real McCoy* office, Andrea called the meeting of the R.M.S.I.U. to order promptly at 3:15 PM. I sat across from Lance, who had the bright-eyed look of a little boy who is just bursting to show his classmates what he'd brought into show-and-tell. I had my own bit of news to share, but I wasn't eager to tell it and I wasn't sure anyone would like to hear it.

Andrea leaned forward and rested her fingertips on the table. "Okay, Lance," she said, "I can see you're eager to get started. Let's take a look at that yearbook."

Lance opened his knapsack and pulled out a large album-sized book that had the words "Witherspoon College" printed in big letters on the cover. The book seemed to be in pretty good condition for something that was over fifteen years old.

"This is Oliver Truitt's yearbook for his freshman year," the Twerp said as he thumbed through the pages.

"You're sure he didn't have a senior yearbook?" Andrea asked.

"No. He flunked out of Witherspoon in his sophomore year and went to another college, in Alaska. I figure if we need to get more information, all we have to do is track down some of the people listed in this book—the way we did with Oliver Truitt—and get their testimony."

"Good thinking, Lance," Andrea said.

"Okay, it's right here!" Lance said abruptly, stopping at a page halfway through the book. He turned the book around so that Andrea and I could see it. "This is what Mr. Karch looked like in his freshman year of college."

The page was filled with black-and-white portraits of the freshman class. Under Mr. Karch's photo, there were two lines that read: GAYLORD KARCH—MAJOR: MATHEMATICS. ACTIVITIES: GLEE CLUB. Studying his picture, I was amazed at how little Mr. Karch had changed over the years. The young Mr. Karch's hair was darker and fuller, and there were fewer lines on his forehead. But the man in the yearbook photo had already developed that same cold look and unsmiling expression that would later strike terror in the hearts of all ninth-grade math students at Wellbie High. I actually found myself feeling sorry for Mr. Karch. I wondered if he'd ever had a chance to be just a regular kid. Did he ever have a crush on a girl or trade baseball cards or dream of the day when he'd be old enough to get his driver's license? They say one picture is worth a thousand words. Right now, I was wishing that Mr. Karch's silent photo could speak just a few.

Andrea interrupted my thoughts. "That's Mr. Karch all right," she said, beaming with satisfaction. "This gives us enough evidence to place him at Witherspoon. It's not enough to show that he graduated, but it's enough to make everybody sit up and take notice. The question is, what do we do next?"

"Let's take it to Mr. Buxton," Lance said brightly.

"You're forgetting about that piece of blotter with Mr. Buxton's name on it," Andrea said. "What if Mr. Buxton is behind all of this?"

"Oh yeah," Lance said. "Better forget that idea."

I shifted uneasily in my seat. It was time to drop my bombshell.

"I can't say for absolute sure," I began, "but I don't think Mr. Buxton's involved at all."

Andrea and Lance looked at me with surprise.

"What? How do you know that, Willi?"

I took a deep breath. "Well, I think I know who took Mr. Karch's records."

Andrea sat down with a thud that made her glasses bounce on her nose. She was speechless for a second, then started barraging me with questions. "Who? Why? How'd you find out?" she asked.

Now came the hardest part. "I can't say," I said.

Andrea stared at me incredulously. "What do you mean, you can't say?" she said, practically choking on her words. "First you tell us that you've solved the biggest mystery in Wellbie history and now you tell us that you can't let us in on the secret?"

"I'm sorry," I said, "but I can't."

"I demand to know why not," Andrea sputtered.

"I've got to protect my sources. If I revealed any more information, somebody could get into real deep trouble. And at this moment, there's still a chance of making things better without anybody else getting hurt."

"You mean, you can't even tell *us*?" asked Lance.

"Not even you," I replied sadly. "I'm in a delicate position here. I don't want to betray my sources. Surely you guys can understand that."

Andrea fumed for a while in silence, then said, "Okay, let me get this straight, Willi. Are you saying that you've got the scoop, but we don't get a story out of it?"

"Not quite. We can still go ahead with a story based on the yearbook information, because nobody's come up with that yet. That's our scoop, and we can run it as our lead in next week's paper. But we can't get into the question of who took the records."

"So what do you propose to do with that information?"

"Give me a little time—until next week's paper comes out—and I think this whole case will solve itself."

Andrea and Lance gave me baffled looks.

"You've got to trust me on this," I implored.

"Okay," said Andrea, "You've got your time. I appreciate your concern for your sources. But if somebody else gets the story and outscoops us in the meantime, I'll never forgive you."

* * *

On Friday, Jennifer and I wandered over to the gym after school to watch Robbie Wilton wrestle against Stockton Regional, our big rival for the state interscholastic championships. It was a welcome change of pace for me. This had been one of the most hectic weeks of my life, and I had no clear sense that I'd made the right decisions about anything. Once again, I found myself in the peculiar position of not being able to share my troubles with my best friend, because they involved my work as "Dear Heart." It had happened last fall, when Bucky wrote to "Dear Heart" that he had a deep crush on Jennifer. And it happened again a few months later when Jennifer publicly attacked my column and asked *me* to help her run "Jennifer's Corner." In both cases, I felt like I was trapped in a bad dream—the kind where you try to cry out for help, but no sound comes out of your mouth. At times like these, I wished I'd never heard of "Dear Heart," because it forced me to keep so many secrets from so many people—including people I loved.

Unlike me, Jennifer was bubbling with good news. En route to the gym, she told me that her dad had mentioned to her that he liked Jim a lot.

"You know," Jennifer said, "Dad's been away so much, he's never had a chance to get to know Jim. Tuesday was the first time they had more than ten minutes together, and they hit it off real well."

"That's great," I said "But how about your dad and Leona? Are they still hitting it off?"

"Not so well—that's the really good news. It seems that Dad called Leona on Wednesday for some reason or another and got the answering machine. When Tessa got home, she checked the tape, heard Dad's message and "accidentally" erased it to keep her mom from returning Dad's call. What she didn't know was that Mrs. Ramsey had already heard Dad's message and apparently wasn't too interested in calling him back anyway. In fact, Mrs. Ramsey told Tessa that if Dad called again, she should tell him that she wasn't home."

"Sounds to me like a romance on the rocks. What do you think could have happened between them?"

"I don't know, but whatever it is, it's wonderful. And the best part is that Tessa told me this morning that Mrs. Ramsey is going out with Ken Pitt tonight!"

"The most eligible lawyer in town?"

"Uh-huh."

"Well," I said, "What a nice turn of events—and none too soon."

"Right. Tomorrow our truce expires and Tessa and I can go back to being enemies again."

"Ah, sweet hostility," I said.

At the wrestling match, we met Bucky and Jim in the bleachers and together we watched the Wellbie Wolverines trounce the Stockton Steelers 6 to 2. Robbie won his match in the last twenty seconds with a dramatic reversal and pin that brought the house down. Jennifer and I cheered until we were hoarse. The Wolverine victory had put us into the state championships for sure. I felt happy for Robbie and our team, but unhappy for me, because it meant that I'd probably have to suffer through another Robbie-less month while he kept in training for the championships. The Gaylord Karch investigation had already made a wreck of my social life. Robbie's wrestling schedule was ensuring that I'd become an old maid before my time.

After the match, Jennifer, Robbie, Jim, Bucky, and I went over to the Caboose Diner to celebrate. The Twerp was working behind the counter again, and he got his dad to give us all free ice cream. It felt like old times again. I temporarily forgot about Emma and Turk and my endangered promotion. For this evening, at least, I was going to celebrate with my friends and put all my worries aside.

Chapter 14

On Saturday, Duke, Jennifer, and I saw Mr. Barnes off at the Wellbie Airport. It was a tearful but triumphant moment for Jennifer because she finally realized that she would never have to worry about the Leona problem again. On Friday night, when she'd screwed up her courage to ask, Mr. Barnes had told her that he'd never been deeply interested in Mrs. Ramsey. He certainly liked Leona's company, he said. But their personalities were much too different to ever lead to anything serious. And he had a good laugh when Jennifer confessed to him that she thought they had really been sweet on each other.

"Where did you get that crazy idea?" he asked.

"Would you believe a fortune cookie?" she replied, and Mr. Barnes had given her a puzzled look.

After Mr. Barnes's jet took off, Duke drove us back to town in his Jeep for a very important appointment. At precisely high noon, he dropped us off at the town square. We stood in the shadow of a tall bronze statue of Wanda McCoy Wellbie, the city founder and Andrea's great-grandmother.

It was a spectacular Iowa day, cold but clear-skied. I was glad I had on my new down jacket to insulate me from the cutting winds blowing down from the roller-coastery hills. Two blocks down on Main Street, I saw a limousine stop. A chauffeur got out and walked around to the side doors. Standing smartly at attention, he opened the doors and let Andrea and Tessa out. Bundled in long, expensive-looking coats, the two girls walked toward us with a sense of high purpose. When they reached the square, Andrea marched directly over to Jennifer and halted in front of her.

"Congratulations, Jennifer," she said, extending her hand. "You kept your agreement."

"You, too, Tessa," I said, shaking Tessa's hand. "I know it was hard."

Tessa shrugged.

"Now, there's just one small matter to conclude," Andrea said, pulling a piece of paper out of the inside of her coat. It was the contract that Tessa and Jennifer had signed at The Caboose Diner. Andrea placed the document in a little cavity at the feet of her great-grandmother's statue.

"Allow me," said Jennifer, pulling a book of matches out of her pocket. She lit a match and touched it to the edge of the paper. Tongues of fire began eating away at the contract, causing it to curl and blacken in the fanning wind.

"I hereby declare the Truce of the Caboose to be over," pronounced Andrea.

"You know," I ventured, "this doesn't mean we *have* to go back to the way things were. We could sort of *try* to be friendlier toward one another. What do you say?"

"Not on your life, sweetie," Tessa said. "There isn't enough room in all of Wellbie for Jennifer *and* me."

"Oh, but there would be, sweetie," Jennifer shot back, "if you could only stick to your diet."

Tessa glared at Jennifer.

Jennifer glowered back at Tessa.

Andrea and I looked at each other and shook our heads. Trying to get Jennifer and Tessa to make a permanent peace was as futile as trying to beat back the ocean waves. Tessa would always be Tessa, and Jennifer would always be Jennifer—and the two of them would never mix.

Andrea and I burst out laughing simultaneously. Everything was back to normal again.

On the Friday after Mr. Barnes left, the momentous issue of *The Real McCoy* came out. It contained my front-page story on the Karch case ("NEW EVIDENCE BACKS MR. KARCH'S CLAIMS") and the "Dear Heart" reply to Emma. This time around, Andrea and I played it safe and made sure that Mr. Purdy and Mr. Buxton saw a copy of the Karch article a couple of days before we actually published it. We didn't want to cause another blow-up like the one that took place over "Trivia On Toast." At first, Mr. Buxton was angered by what we did and accused us of violating our promise not to get involved. But then, as he read the article, his mood changed completely. I think he quickly realized that Lance and I had turned up genuinely new information—information that required further investigation by the school board. In fact, by the time Andrea and I left his office, he was praising our work to the skies, saying that Andrea, Lance, and I should be proud of ourselves—that we were a credit to the school. Imagine that!

Our meeting with Mr. Buxton set off a chain reaction. Mr. Buxton immediately notified the school board, and the school board promptly re-opened its investigation. By the time *The Real McCoy* appeared on Friday, our story had become big news. Andrea, Lance, and I even got inter-viewed on TV by Deirdre Carruthers of Action NewsCenter 6.

My "Dear Heart" column had an equally impor-tant impact on events, although no one ever knew it but me—and, of course, Emma. Emma must have read my reply to her letter and acted on it, because on the following Monday morn-ing, Mr. Karch's missing documents mysteriously reappeared—in, of all places, Mr. Buxton's office. As Mr. Buxton sheepishly told reporters later, the records had been found peeking out from under the blotter on his desk. He confessed that he couldn't explain how they got there, but he imagined (with some embarrassment) that they must have gotten lost under there during a recent reorganization of the office filing system. He guessed that a cleaning woman had probably knocked the blotter out of kilter on Friday night, exposing the documents. According to Mr. Buxton, the recovery of Mr. Karch's records had "closed the case against Gaylord Karch." He added that Mr. Karch would receive a public apology and be permitted to return to the classroom immediately.

He returned, surprisingly, as a slightly mellower man—someone who seemed to have actually learned something from his awful ordeal. Oh, don't get me wrong. He didn't let up on us one bit. Math still "marched on," and we still had to go through those terrifying monthly Math Bees. But math seemed to march on a little bit more mercifully, and Mr. Karch seemed to act with just a little bit more respect for his students' feelings. It wasn't quite as amazing a conversion as Scrooge's in *A Christmas Carol*, but it was enough of a change in heart to increase our appreciation of him. And to tell the truth, after being subjected to a month of bewildering instruction from "Better Math Through Better Breathing" LaRue, most of us in seventh-period algebra class would have been ready to welcome back the old Karch. And, oh yes, Mr. Karch did win that MATTY award, which he displayed proudly in his classroom.

Things turned out well for Emma, too. About a week after our story broke, I picked up the following letter from the "Dear Heart" box:

Dear Heart:
  Thank you for your help. Because of you I was able to help someone in my

family get out of trouble. I was also able to talk to him for the first time and tell him how I felt about what he did. I cried, and even he cried, and we're much closer now. I love you, Dear Heart.

No Longer Broken Up

And me?

After the sensational success of our article on Mr. Karch, Andrea gave Lance and me our promotions. Lance was elevated to the position of "senior editor," and my new title on the masthead became "Wilhelmina Stevens, investigative reporter." When I got Andrea alone, I asked her if that meant I would be giving up "Dear Heart."

She turned to me and said, "Not on your life. You're too good to lose in that job."

When I told Jennifer about my promotion to investigative reporter, she leaped for joy.

"Can you tell me what your first assignment is?" she asked.

"You'll never believe it," I said.

"C'mon give," she teased.

"The cafeteria lunch crisis."

Jennifer looked at me, and we both laughed.